KU-531-493

THE CAPTAIN'S WIFE

1975. After years struggling to cope with a childless marriage and the loneliness of being left behind while her seafaring husband Max is away, Sarah finally persuades him to take her with him on a four-month voyage. But she is not prepared for the change in him once in command of his ship, and often feels resentful that he has so little time for her. Over the months she and Geoffrey, the chief officer, are drawn together for comfort, and perhaps more — but is that what Sarah really wants?

JEAN ROBINSON

THE CAPTAIN'S WIFE

Complete and Unabridged

LINFORD
Leicester

First published in Great Britain in 2013

First Linford Edition
published 2014

Copyright © 2013 by Jean Robinson
All rights reserved

A catalogue record for this book is available
from the British Library.

ISBN 978–1–4448–2192–5

MORAY COUNCIL
DEPARTMENT OF TECHNICAL
& LEISURE SERVICES
ʄ

20295430

Published by
F. A. Thorpe (Publishing)
Anstey, Leicestershire

Set by Words & Graphics Ltd.
Anstey, Leicestershire
Printed and bound in Great Britain by
T. J. International Ltd., Padstow, Cornwall

This book is printed on acid-free paper

1

Leaving Liverpool

Sarah stood on the balcony looking out on the September landscape. The silver birch was swaying in the breeze, fallen leaves already rustling in the courtyard below. Beyond the wall, russet hues were replacing the summer greenery in the woods. Soon it would be winter and then Christmas — another one without Max. 1975 would pass into history and again Max would not be at her side to celebrate.

At least there was a new baby in the family this year. Her sister was a great mum to her ever-growing brood. Giles was a beautiful baby and Sarah adored him. But he wasn't her baby.

Max came up behind her. 'Sarah, it's freezing out here. Come back inside.'

She turned and reached up to kiss

her husband. He took her in his arms and she felt his familiar warmth encircle her. Then he led her back into the apartment. 'It will soon pass,' he said.

She so much wanted to believe him, but the ache in her heart denied it. How would she cope with more months without Max? It became harder every time.

'At least this trip will be shorter. Now the Suez Canal's open again we can knock weeks off the voyage.'

He stood in front of her, straight and tall, a handsome man with fine features and those deep dark eyes that never failed to stir her. Always positive. Sarah didn't know how he did it. However hard she tried, the pain wouldn't let her see it that way. As his eyes searched hers they were deep with passion.

'How long will you be gone?' She tried to keep the tremor from her voice.

'Three and a half months, maybe a bit more.'

She swallowed. How much more? He

always tried to make it sound less.

From the way Max was looking at her she knew, deep down, his feelings were as raw as hers. He took both her hands in his and a tremor of longing rippled through her. 'Why don't you come with me next trip?'

She blinked in bewilderment. 'What? You want me to come with you?'

He straightened and a shadow passed over his face. 'Sarah, I have always wanted you with me. But I don't think you know what you're letting yourself in for.'

Her heart was thumping in her chest. Max wanted her to go with him.

He gave her hands a squeeze. 'Cargo ships aren't cruise liners. You'll be on holiday. But I won't.' He paused and swallowed. 'We could give it a try if you want to.'

A beam spread across her face as she realized what he was saying. 'Of course I want to. It's what I've always wanted.' She flung her arms round his neck. 'Oh, Max, I can't bear the thought of you going off in a couple of days' time and leaving me again for months on end.'

His frown merged into a smile. 'Let's open that bottle of champagne we didn't drink when Giles was born.'

As she watched him pull the cork, she did a quick calculation. There would be so much to arrange in such a short time. But she would do it. She would do anything to be with Max.

She took the glass from him and walked over to the fire to warm herself. Max came to join her. 'That Six-Day War back in sixty-seven. I was a junior officer then. We had a lucky escape, you know. Fourteen ships stranded when Nasser put up the blockades. Stuck there for eight years, they were. Called them the Yellow Fleet. Caused a big furore. That canal's our gateway to the Far East. Make a big difference now it's open again.'

She looked up at him, the smile still on her face. Her husband was a seaman through and through. Everything came second to his ship. But she was too happy and excited to resent that now.

Max wanted her to go with him. There would be no heart-rending goodbye this time when he went off. She would be there by his side.

* * *

Three days later, on a chilly September afternoon, Sarah followed Max up the gangway of the Melbourne and wondered if it really was a good idea or whether Max had been right all along.

He'd always maintained that a cargo ship on a long voyage out to the Far East was a man's world and that she would probably be the only woman amongst a crew of fifty-odd men. She'd tried so often to persuade him to take her with him — had even given up her teaching job to please him, in the hope that one day he would relent. But he never had. Now, out of the blue, he'd agreed. Tomorrow they would be sailing down the Mersey and this ship would be her home for the next three-and-a-half months.

The Liverpool dockside was buzzing with activity. Forklift trucks lumbered around, moving cargo. Cranes crunched and grated as they turned on their metal swivels, heaving crates of cargo into the holds of ships alongside the quay. Men shouted across to each other above the grinding, clanking noise of machinery and constant drone of motors.

Officers in uniform high above them on the deck of the *Melbourne* directed operations. The smells of tar and engine oil permeated the air. It was frightening and exciting, and a far cry from the quiet Cheshire village where Sarah lived with Max.

Lived with Max! It was how Sarah always thought of it. After two years of marriage, she still couldn't think of his smart apartment as her home. It was large, modern and comfortable, but it wasn't hers. She longed for a back door leading to a garden where children could play and maybe a dog. But Max had made it quite clear he wanted none of it. Well, if this ship was Max's world, she was determined to share it with him.

They made their way along narrow alleyways and up ladders until they reached the captain's deck just below the bridge. Max unlocked the door into his accommodation and stood back to allow her to step inside. This was one of the company's larger ships and, as captain, Max had the quarterdeck below the bridge to himself. The room was spacious, furnished with a desk and comfy-looking chairs and a settee. There were book shelves, a coffee table and nice table lamps. Max watched as she took it all in.

He swung open a heavy weather door onto a section of deck. 'There you are, your own private deck. You can sit there all day and nobody will disturb you.'

Two cane chairs stood beside a round table and a couple of deckchairs were stowed alongside the bulkhead. Sarah couldn't imagine using them in this chilly weather but knew that once they were in the tropics they would come into their own. Her heart did a dance at the thought of sitting out there with Max, sipping gin and tonic as the ship gently glided through the water. And this little deck would give her some privacy on a ship full of men.

Max was already at his desk, rustling through papers and opening mail. He was on the phone asking questions and giving orders. There was no time to settle in. He was on the job immediately. Someone tapped at the open door and whatever it was sounded urgent.

'Have to go, love. I have to relieve Captain Banks. He's anxious to get off so we need to do the hand-over as quickly as possible. The trunks should be up any minute so you'll be able to unpack.' With that he was gone.

She wandered around, examining everything. The bedroom was a good size with a big double bunk and some fitted cupboards, and off that was a shower room.

She looked through the thick glass portholes at the activity on the quay and felt almost dizzy. From the top deck of this huge ship it seemed as if she were viewing the scene from a tower. Tomorrow they'd be sailing down the Mersey and out into the Irish Sea, and that buzz of excitement gripped her again.

After half an hour there was still no sign of Max or the cabin trunks, so she stepped outside onto the deck and peered over the rail at the activity on the water. Small tug boats were manoeuvring a ship away from the dockside and the roar of engines was deafening. It edged from its berth and into the middle of the dock and then down towards the open river. Those little tug boats were so powerful.

Back inside, she looked for some means of making a cup of tea. Max had told her to ring for anything she wanted. As her finger hovered over the bell there was a tap at the door and a smart young man in a steward's uniform stood there with a tray. He smiled at her, put the tray of tea and biscuits down on the coffee table and introduced himself as Joe. She looked at it in amazement then at Joe. 'You must be a mind-reader. I was gasping for a cup of tea.'

'Is there anything else I can get for you?' he asked.

'No, that looks perfect.'

He was on his way out but she wanted to be friendly. 'Do you live locally, Joe? I think I detect a Liverpool accent.'

He turned and smiled at her. 'Used to live in Bootle but I got married last year and me and the wife got a flat in Ainsdale.'

'I have a sister who lives there. Is your wife on board?'

'No, Jen's expecting.'

There was pride is his voice and Sarah smiled. 'You must miss her.'

'I do. But that's the life, isn't it? Better get back. It's chaos in the galley today. I'll be glad when we sail.'

Max appeared briefly to collect some papers and to make sure she was all right. 'Steward looking after you, I see. That's good.' He rummaged in a drawer, found what he was looking for, then straightened up to face her. 'At least you have company this voyage. We have two other wives on board and a nine-year-old child.'

Sarah felt a glow of happiness. She'd have female company. She wouldn't be the only woman on the ship after all. And a child would liven things up. Max didn't look too pleased, so she kept her feelings to herself.

Work had stopped now and the dockside was quiet, so she went exploring. There were several ladders to go down before she reached a lower deck where there was room to walk. A small girl came skipping along, singing to herself, and nearly collided with Sarah, then stopped dead just ahead of her and looked up. She had startled blue eyes in a pretty face, blonde hair and a fresh complexion, and was dainty and simply dressed in jeans and sweater.

'Hello,' Sarah said. 'And what's your name?'

The girl backed away but didn't take her eyes off Sarah. 'My name's Jessica but you can call me Jess. Everyone does. Except Mummy, and she only calls me Jessica when she's cross with me.'

Sarah smiled. 'Well, Jess, that's a very nice skipping rope you've got.'

'Not bad,' Jess agreed, looking at it. 'Geoffrey made it for me. I forgot to bring one with me. Mummy said it's a good thing to do on a ship 'cos you can't do much else.'

'You'll be able to swim once we get to sea and they fill the pool.'

'I can't swim,' Jess said.

'Well, you'll have to learn this voyage.'

'How do I do that? Mummy said not to go near it 'cos it's very deep. And Daddy doesn't swim. How can I learn if I can't stand up? I'd drown before I learnt.'

Sarah smiled at the logic in this. Jess

was obviously a bright child.

'Can you swim?' Jess asked her.

'Yes, I love the water.'

'Will you teach me?'

'What about Mummy? Doesn't she swim, either?'

'She doesn't like getting her hair messed up. Will you?' Jess persisted.

'Of course I will. Have you been on a ship before, Jess?'

'Loads of times. My dad's the chief steward. But I've never been on a long voyage.'

'Neither have I. Are you looking forward to it?'

'I'd rather be at school.'

Sarah laughed.

'Can you skip?' Jess asked her.

'I think so.' Sarah wasn't sure. It had been a long time since she'd tried. 'May I have a go?' She reached for the rope.

Jess handed it to her. It looked like an old piece of ship's rope which had been intricately plaited and woven to form handles. Geoffrey was obviously a dab hand with his nautical knots. She tried a few quick turns of the rope and managed not to trip up. Then she stopped for breath and realized she wasn't as fit as she used to be.

'You're good,' Jess said.

'Very impressive,' came a deep voice from behind her. She turned and found herself looking into a pair of laughing blue eyes. He was tall and tanned and looked quite amazing in his crisp white shirt and dark navy uniform with all the gold braid.

'Geoffrey Golder,' he said, offering his hand. 'Chief officer, or should I say chief dogsbody! Pleased to meet you, Mrs Wilson.'

Sarah shook his hand and the grip was firm and warm. 'Sarah, please,' she said.

'Geoffrey made my skipping rope,' Jess piped up.

'And I'm pleased it's getting such good use.' Geoffrey winked at Sarah and a strange warm feeling made her feel this ship was a good place to be. She smiled and handed the rope back to Jess. 'Enough for one day.'

Geoffrey continued along the deck and Jess skipped after him. Sarah watched them until they disappeared out of sight and found she was still smiling.

Max was waiting when she got back to the room. 'Ah, there you are. The trunks are in the bedroom so you can unpack later, then we can get them locked away in the store room. I thought we could go down to the bar before dinner and meet everyone.'

He'd changed into his uniform and she felt pride swell in her. The cut, the gold braided cuffs, the crisp white shirt and black tie against his tanned skin. He carried it off so well. Sometimes she had to pinch herself to believe this handsome man really was her husband.

'Just give me ten minutes to make myself look respectable.'

'Sarah, you always look wonderful.' He pulled her towards him and brushed her lips softly, sending a ripple of desire through her. But he was already looking at his watch, so she quickly changed into a green princess-line dress that skimmed her hips and showed off her slim waist. The colour complemented her dark hair and brown eyes and she felt good. She wanted to look a credit to Max.

The bar, at one end of the officers' lounge, was crowded when they went in. The men, all formally dressed in uniform, stood up to greet her. Both the other wives were sitting with drinks and, after the introductions, she sat in the proffered seat next to the chief engineer, George, while Max went to get drinks from the bar.

George was a hearty sort who kept the conversation going and everyone laughing. Sarah sat quietly enjoying a large gin and tonic and trying to work out who was who. Geoffrey didn't appear and she tried not to be disappointed.

Nancy sat beside her husband, Malcolm, who, by the two stripes on his jacket sleeve, was obviously the second officer. She was young and slim, dressed in a simple Laura Ashley dress without jewellery or make-up, long straight hair framing her pretty face. Malcolm tried to bring her into the conversation but she sat quietly composed with her hands in her lap.

Maggie was a large woman with shoulder-length curly hair. She wore a patterned silky dress, cut low and clinging to her ample figure. With a cigarette in one hand and a gin and tonic in the other, she lolled back in her seat and laughed loudly at George's jokes, then competed with stories of her own of voyages she'd done. An old-timer, Sarah thought.

All eyes turned when a vivacious redhead walked into the bar. She wore a uniform and looked strikingly attractive.

'Ah, here comes our pretty young cadet,' George guffawed. 'Come along in, Shelly, and join us.'

Shelly blushed and gave an embarrassed laugh.

'And who's the lucky officer to have

that young lady on watch with him?' he boomed as he watched her walk towards the bar.

Sarah felt uncomfortable and glanced at Max. But he was in conversation and hadn't heard the comment.

Malcolm got up. 'Behave, George,' he said without smiling as he walked past him.

'Ah, it's our Malcolm, is it?' Then he turned to Nancy. 'You watch that husband of yours, my dear. Up on the bridge at night with a pretty young cadet.' He raised an eyebrow and laughed out loud. 'Well, well, I never!'

Nancy wasn't laughing. She looked tense and kept glancing towards the bar where Malcolm was getting drinks. Sarah wished George would keep his opinions to himself. He obviously wasn't the sensitive type and it was clear he didn't approve of the company's new policy of introducing female cadets on board any more than Max did.

Malcolm came back with the drinks and put one in front of Nancy. She stared at it and then glanced back to the bar where Shelly was now chatting with Will, one of the engineer cadets.

When the gong went for dinner, Max strode ahead and into the dining saloon, where he took up his position at the top of the centre table. A smartly-dressed steward pulled a chair out next to him for Sarah, then the other officers took their places in the room. There was a table either side where the more junior officers sat and each was laid formally with a crisp white tablecloth, silver cutlery and sparkling glasses.

Sarah studied the menu while one of the stewards stood behind waiting for her order. She chose the smoked salmon for starters and Max ordered soup.

Sarah noticed that Maggie and Jess hadn't come in.

'They come to first sitting,' Max said. 'I won't have a child in the saloon when I'm dining.'

Sarah wasn't surprised but she didn't like his tone. 'The child has a name,' she said quietly.

'I expect she does. But that is no concern of mine. So long as her mother keeps her out of my way then all will be well.'

The conversation drifted round the table as the meal was served. The food was excellent, with plenty of choice at each course.

'I shall go home a stone heavier,' Sarah joked with George.

'Aye, you'll have to watch it, lass. They feed you well, they do, on these ships.' He contemplated his steak, patted his very substantial stomach and chuckled loudly.

2

Lonely Days

Next day Sarah stood out on deck as they sailed down the Mersey. A ferryboat was ploughing its way across to New Brighton. All along the banks were stacks of cargo, cranes and ships manoeuvring in and out of docks.

The Mersey pilot left as soon as they reached Holyhead. Sarah watched him scramble down the vertical pilot ladder and into the small pilot boat which had drawn up alongside. Then she joined Max on the bridge as he took the ship out of Holyhead Bay.

It wasn't long before the ship began to pitch and Max turned to make sure she was all right. 'We're entering heavy seas. There's a swell running and a gale forecast. I'm afraid we're in for a rough ride.'

Sarah watched as water began to surge over the decks and the derricks swung alarmingly over the hatches with the motion of the ship. She could see very little through the thickening fog and could hear the foghorn give its eerie call, warning other ships in the vicinity.

Max stood staring ahead, his long-sighted eyes scanning the horizon, his deep steady voice giving orders to the man at the wheel for adjustments to the ship's course: every bit the seaman, in command of his ship just as he was in command of his life.

Sarah stood out of the way, feeling the tension, the way the men worked together to keep the ship on a steady course in such adverse conditions. She was tempted to join Ben, one of the officer cadets, on the bridge wing, but when she saw how he was bracing himself against the wind she decided to stay in the shelter of the wheelhouse.

She wandered over to Geoffrey, who was peering at the radar, and tried to see what he was studying. He turned when he realised she was standing beside him and drew her into view of the screen. The pressure of his hand on her shoulder sent a shiver through her and she was aware of the closeness of his body as he stood behind her, explaining in his easy manner what she was looking at. As she drew away their eyes met and the moment lasted just a little too long. Then he quickly returned to the screen and she moved back to where she'd been standing.

'Dead slow ahead.' The clear voice Max used when navigating calmed her. It was always followed by the monotonous echo from the seaman at the wheel as he repeated the order word for word before cranking the ship's telegraph to send a message to the engine room for a change of speed.

'Once we clear Ushant the weather should calm,' Geoffrey said, looking towards her.

'I hope I'm not in the way,' she said.

His smile sent her pulse racing. 'I

don't think you'd ever be in the way.' And again there was that look.

Sarah didn't mind the storm. She found it exciting and exhilarating. And she liked being on the bridge and part of it all. Geoffrey was right, and the weather did soon calm and a watery sun showed through.

'Heading for Gibraltar now,' Max told her. 'Let's go below and have a drink. I'm ready for one. The mate can take over here.'

Next day the sea was calm, the sky a perfect blue with a gentle warm breeze. After a good night's sleep and a three-course breakfast in the dining saloon, Sarah felt ready for anything. First she needed some exercise, so she put on a warm jacket and began to walk round the deck. She'd managed it three times, then saw Maggie standing at the rail and went to join her.

Maggie, muffled in a large woollen cardigan, wasn't looking happy. 'I don't think your husband likes children, does he?'

Sarah thought how right she was but wasn't going to be disloyal to Max. 'I think he worries about them being on board a ship.'

'Well, he better get used to it. Company policy now. Children over eight are allowed on voyages and there's not a thing he can do about it.'

Sarah didn't like her tone and hoped Maggie wasn't going to talk to Max that way. He would certainly put her in her place.

'Have you done a voyage before?' Maggie asked, looking her up and down.

'No, only a bit of coasting.'

'Thought so. You won't be looking so pleased with yourself in a couple of weeks' time.'

'What do you mean?'

'When you've done as many voyages as I have you'll find out.'

Sarah had no idea what she was talking about.

'You're a teacher, aren't you?' Maggie said.

'I was, but I gave it up when I married Max. We wanted to have time together when he came home on leave. I do a bit of supply work when Max is away.'

Maggie looked at Sarah with interest. 'You could teach Jess. Keep your hand in. I don't want her getting behind at school. She's very clever, you know. It would give you something to do.'

Sarah smiled. 'Well, I haven't been bored so far. There always seems to be something going on. But, yes, I'd be pleased to. She seems a bright child. Don't the school mind you taking her out for so long?'

Maggie turned her gaze out to sea. 'None of their business, is it? She's my child. I do what I want with her. If I say she comes on a voyage with me, then she does. If the powers that be don't like it then hard luck.' She hunched her shoulders and her mouth tightened. 'Anyway, we've taken her out of that school. It didn't suit her. They didn't cater for gifted children like Jess.' She paused then looked back at Sarah questioningly. 'Don't you have any?'

'No.' Sarah didn't want to go into that.

'Don't blame you. I haven't been on a voyage for years because of Jess.'

Jess came running up and Sarah was glad of the distraction. She really didn't want to discuss her private life with someone she had only just met. In fact she couldn't imagine ever wanting to discuss her private life with this woman.

★　★　★

The Bay of Biscay threw up another storm and the ship began to pitch and toss. Even Max was looking a bit green.

'Always get queasy first bad weather we hit,' he told her. 'Lots of seamen do. You'd think we'd get used to it, wouldn't you? Best thing is to get out on deck in the fresh air. Keep your eye on the horizon. Come up on the bridge with me.'

Sarah felt fine but was pleased he wanted her up there with him. She stood on the starboard wing in the open but soon had to seek shelter in the wheelhouse from the strength of the wind. Waves were lashing over the sides and up over the bow as the ship pitched and tossed its way through the spray, and she had to hang on to the ledge to steady herself.

It was exhilarating watching the tall arms of the cranes lurching first to one side then the other as the ship began to roll. Waves buffeted the hatches and crashed on the deck but Sarah had complete confidence in Max as he stood beside the helmsman, keeping the ship on a steady course through the treacherous seas.

When it began to calm Max handed over to Malcolm and stood back with Sarah. 'The new container ships have better stabilizers. You can hardly feel any movement at all, I've been told.'

'How dull,' she said with a twinkle in her eye. 'I find it quite exhilarating.'

Max gave her a bemused look and shook his head.

He paced up and down, listening to each order Malcolm gave, eyes skimming the horizon, and then he looked at the radar. Sarah felt he was checking that his second mate came up to scratch and she smiled to herself. Max left nothing to chance.

The storm cleared as fast as it had sprung up and Max handed her the binoculars and pointed. 'There, look, you can see the Rock of Gibraltar.'

'I can't see any apes,' she laughed.

'They're there all right,' he said.

★ ★ ★

As the ship made steady progress through the Mediterranean, life on board settled into a routine. Sarah loved the time she spent with Max, when he'd stand beside her and point out places on the distant coastline, or they'd go for a swim, or sit and talk. At these times he seemed relaxed and happy to have her with him. But all too often he would be called away to deal with some problem. If they hit bad weather he could be up on the bridge all night and then doze in his chair during the day. Other times he'd seem preoccupied and she felt he hardly noticed she was there.

Much of the time she sat in the warm sun and watched the coastline changing from the mountains of southern Spain to the rugged coast of north Africa, or she would lean over the rail watching the bow waves skimming the hull. The constant throb of the ship's engine vibrating through the deck and the smell of engine oil and tar were so familiar to her now she hardly noticed them. Time seemed irrelevant and she could never remember being so idle.

★　★　★

Maggie was sorting through the ship's supply of films when Sarah went into the lounge to change her library book. She looked up at Sarah from the floor where she was crouched over a pile of tapes. 'Look at this lot.'

'Anything interesting?' Sarah said. 'I believe we're having a film show tonight.'

'Nothing at all. *Blazing Saddles, The Towering Inferno, The Godfather.* We're not all interested in westerns and crime.'

Sarah shrugged. 'I suppose most of the men are.'

Maggie gave her a withering look, shoved the pile back in the cupboard and stalked out of the room. Sarah pulled a face at her back and smothered a snort of laughter.

When she mentioned it to Geoffrey he laughed out loud. There were just the two of them by the pool and she was about to get into the water as he was getting out.

He stood dripping on the side, his muscles glistening in the sunlight. 'She does like to organise things to suit her. Thinks she's on a cruise liner.' He reached for a towel and watched Sarah dip her toe in the water.

She eased herself down the ladder into the canvas pool. 'This ship does feel a bit like that. Not that I've been on a cruise liner, but I wasn't expecting this sort of luxury.'

'We used to carry passengers at one time. Just a few. Business men, mainly, who didn't like flying, and retired couples with money who wanted to travel by sea but didn't want bingo and keep-fit.'

Sarah laughed as she clung onto the side, watching him drying off. 'I don't blame them. I don't think I'd fancy that, either.' Then she was wistful. 'It would be nice to see a bit more of Max, though.'

His expression changed. 'Neglecting you, is he?'

She shrugged. 'There's always someone knocking on the door. Then he disappears and I don't see him for hours. We hardly ever have time together.'

He smiled at her. 'I'll go and chase him down from the bridge, shall I?'

She gave him a grateful nod and her eyes followed him until he was out of sight.

* * *

Max took Sarah ashore in Genoa while the ship was berthed alongside, loading cargo and taking on bunkers. He bought her a lovely cameo bracelet, and then they went for a meal in a tiny restaurant he knew. They didn't stay ashore long as Max seemed anxious to get back to the ship. But it was good to get him away for a short time and feel he was hers and not always worried about what was happening on board.

* * *

As they headed for the Suez Canal her excitement grew. She'd heard a lot about the Middle East on the news and remembered vaguely about the war and the closure of the canal eight years ago. It would be interesting to see where it all happened.

Sitting on the deck outside their room, deep in thought, she was startled when the klaxon sounded, and then she remembered Max had warned her there would be a lifeboat drill this morning.

Putting on her lifejacket, she made her way to one of the starboard lifeboats where she'd been told to muster. The crew were already working the davits to lower the boat and Sarah watched with interest as it swung out over the water.

Nancy stood a distance from them, quietly alone in a simple cotton dress and sandals. Sarah had seen little of her since joining the ship. Malcolm said she was shy and reserved and preferred to keep herself to herself; she found it difficult to mix.

Maggie, as usual, was complaining bitterly. Her hair was wet and she was struggling to fasten her lifejacket, with Jess trying to help. 'All this fuss. We know the routine by now. I was in the middle of washing my hair and I get dragged out on deck for all this performance.'

Geoffrey was checking names off his list and heard her. 'If we had an engine room fire and it got out of control you'd be glad we had it well rehearsed.' He gave Sarah a knowing smile and she muffled a giggle. It silenced Maggie but she still looked disgruntled.

When they'd finished, Sarah walked over to Nancy. 'You wouldn't sleep through that klaxon, would you?'

'It is rather noisy but I suppose it has to be.' Nancy averted her eyes and unfastened her lifejacket. She had slim hands with short, neat nails. She always looked so natural with her long, silky hair and tall, slim figure — never any make-up or jewellery, just simple shift dresses or flowing skirts. She was already moving away and Sarah shook her head as she watched her go back inside. It would be so nice if they could be friends.

She dumped her lifejacket back in the room and set off on her morning walk round the deck. Maggie caught up with her and they stopped and faced each other. 'I want a word with you.'

Sarah groaned inwardly when she

saw the look on Maggie's face.

'I don't know how I'm supposed to manage in that tiny cabin. Half the room's taken up with the spare mattress. Why can't Jess have a room to herself? I know there are empty cabins.'

'Isn't she a bit young to be separated from you?' Sarah wanted to pacify her so she wouldn't hassle Max again.

'She has her own room at home. You're all right up there. You've got a whole suite of rooms just for the two of you. Then there's me and Kevin squashed up with Jess in one room. It's not good enough.'

'I'll talk to Max about it if you like. I'm sure, if there is a spare cabin, she could have it.'

Maggie huffed. 'Don't bother. I'll sort it myself. Kevin's useless. He won't lift a finger. Keeps telling me we can manage and that he doesn't want me making a fuss.'

'Max tells me the same.'

'Oh yes!' There was an edge of sarcasm to her voice. 'You don't know you're born up there. Everyone kow-towing to you.'

Sarah stopped her. 'Maggie, it's not my fault that I have a bigger room than you. I'd be quite content to have a room like yours.'

Maggie gave a snort. 'I'm sure you would!' She paused for effect, then continued her tirade. 'He won't have us in the dining room when he's eating. What is it with your husband and kids?' Then a sneer contorted her face. 'Of course you don't have any, do you? So he won't be used to them.'

A mixture of pain and anger shot through Sarah. She tried to swallow through the tightness in her throat but knew no words would come out. She gave Maggie a withering look and turned away to pound the decks until the thumping in her chest subsided. Then she leant over the rail and let the rhythm of the sea calm her. Once she felt in control again she went in search of Max. She needed his comforting presence. He was putting on his uniform cap when she went into the room.

'Max, where are you off to? Can't you stay with me for a while? I haven't seen you all morning.'

He gave her an apologetic look and made towards the door. 'Sorry, love, can't.'

'Max!' she shouted. 'I want to talk to you.'

He looked alarmed. 'Sarah, I have Inspection in ten minutes. Can't it wait?'

She sighed and flopped down on the settee. He hesitated, then left the room.

After sitting immobile for some minutes, she got up and went back out on deck. She was being unreasonable, she knew. Inspection took place every morning and she usually enjoyed watching this ritual — officers in uniform parading round after the captain, making sure all was shipshape. But today she needed Max to give her some attention instead of expending it all on his ship.

The sky was a perfect blue, the sun warm. The gentle lapping of the waves against the bow of the ship as it ploughed through the water was sooth- ing, the vastness of the sea calming. A sudden feeling of homesickness over- came her as she thought of her sister and her close friends at home. She missed the easy companionship; the gossip. Although she was here with Max, she felt very alone.

For a long time she stared out across the ocean, thinking of home, thinking of her life with Max, wondering how she was to cope with the loneliness. She hadn't expected to feel it here on board with him, but it was almost worse than when they were on opposite sides of the world. At least then she could believe he was missing her and loved her. Now she wasn't sure.

Sarah had been so deep in thought she hadn't noticed Geoffrey standing beside her. He smiled down at her and immediately she felt better.

'Missing home?' he asked.

She looked into his kind blue eyes and nodded.

'We all get that at times during a voyage.'

'I know. But I shouldn't. I'm here with Max. But he's different on board. He hardly notices me. In fact I often think he'd rather I wasn't here at all.' She stopped. Why was she pouring her heart out to someone she barely knew?

His deep calm voice was comforting. 'I'm sure that's not true. It's a big responsibility being the master of a ship like this. He can't switch off. He was up on the bridge all last night with bad weather and he has to sleep sometimes.'

'You think I'm being unreasonable.' She could feel the quiver on her lips and turned away so he wouldn't notice.

'Louise felt the same when she did a trip with me.'

'Would she do another one?' She struggled to keep the tremble out of her voice.

They were standing side by side, looking out across the dark depths of the Mediterranean, sun glinting on the gentle ripples. 'Can't at the moment,' he said. 'The children are too young.'

Her heart contracted. 'I suppose when they're older,' she managed, covering the crack in her voice with a cough.

'I don't think she'd come anyway.' His voice was soft beside her.

Why did her throat feel so tight? Of course Geoffrey would have children. It was what young couples did.

'Louise wants me to get a shore job.'

'Would you do that?'

'No, I couldn't. The sea's my life.'

'Max is the same.' She was struggling to keep her voice normal.

'At least you can do every voyage with Max.'

'I don't think I could. Even if he wanted me to, which I doubt. I've decided to go back to teaching when we get home.' She could hear the quiver in her voice and her lips felt tight.

'No plans for a family, then?'

A stab of pain cut through her. 'Max

doesn't want children.'

'That's a shame. You seem so good with Jess.'

She felt herself welling up. She was going to cry. She mustn't do that. 'She's a lovely child.'

Geoffrey noticed the tremor in her voice and he put his hand over hers. The pressure was comforting and for a moment the pain in her heart quelled.

'You'll feel better once we get through the Suez Canal. It's just this long drag out.'

They stood for some time in companionable silence, each wrapped in their own thoughts. Eventually Geoffrey looked over his shoulder towards where Nancy was settling herself in a deckchair at the opposite side of the ship in the shade. 'She's a strange girl, isn't she? Never talks to anyone.'

Sarah shrugged. 'I've tried but she just walks away.'

'She's very pretty, though, isn't she? In a quiet sort of way.'

'Malcolm said she does every trip

42

with him.' She tried to make her voice sound normal.

Geoffrey laughed. 'She's only done a couple of short ones. They haven't been married long.'

'She's always on the bridge with him when he's on watch.'

Geoffrey nodded. 'I'm surprised your old man hasn't put a stop to that. I wouldn't have thought he'd approve of women on the bridge all the time.'

'I don't think he's too happy about it.'

He raised an eyebrow. 'And Maggie's not exactly your type, either, is she?'

Sarah groaned. 'Not at all. But at least she talks to me.'

He raised an eyebrow. 'Is that a good thing?'

She laughed and Geoffrey squeezed her hand. 'Must go. Duty calls.'

3

Troubled Waters

Sarah walked slowly back across the deck past the swimming pool. Sebastian, the second engineer, was watching Maggie settling herself beside the pool for a session of sunbathing. He was eyeing her up and down and Maggie seemed to be enjoying the attention.

Sarah felt her pace quicken. There was something about him that made her feel uneasy — those heavy eyelids and his sly grin. She climbed the decks, flight by flight, until she reached the top. At the door to their cabin she started as Max banged the phone down on its rest. 'Damned fool! He's never where he ought to be.'

'Who?' Sarah asked.

'The second engineer. Why the company employed him I'll never know.'

'You mean Sebastian? What's wrong?'

Max drew his fingers through his hair and looked at her, his brow creased in a frown. 'Freezers are playing up. Chief steward says he'll have to dump some food. The second engineer should be fixing it.'

'He's by the swimming pool,' Sarah said.

Max's frown deepened. He picked up the phone again and dialled the bridge. 'Send the cadet down to the pool. I want the second engineer up here immediately.'

There was a pause while Max listened. Then he exploded. 'Well, he shouldn't damned well be. What is this, a holiday camp? I want him up here at once.' He slammed down the receiver.

Sarah slipped into the bedroom, picked up her book and escaped through the door. There was going to be trouble and she didn't want to be around when the shouting started. She'd never seen this side of Max before and certainly hadn't been prepared for the change in him once he got on board.

She settled in a deckchair by the rail where she could look out to sea. It was pleasantly warm in the sun and, as her book lay unread on her lap, her thoughts returned to home and her marriage. Something was changing. Max was different. She didn't feel as close to him as she used to.

She tried to remember how she'd felt when she'd first met him six years ago at a friend's birthday party. The confirmed bachelor, Sue had said. He was tall, well built and arrogantly handsome, his brown eyes smiling down at her with obvious interest. She guessed he must have been a bit older than her, in his early thirties. They got on well, talked easily and shared the same sense of humour.

At the end of the party Max had said goodbye most charmingly and disappeared. She'd willed him to phone but he didn't. She'd questioned Sue only to be told he was like that — here today, gone tomorrow. So she organised a get-together in her flat, wheedled his address out of Sue and sent Max an invitation. He accepted.

Then he was off on his ship again and she heard nothing more. She'd almost given up hoping when, months later, he appeared with flowers and an invitation to dinner. They enjoyed a wonderful few weeks together until his leave came to an end. Then off he went and she heard nothing from him again. She told herself many times she should forget about him. But she couldn't. Each time he came home he'd contact her and each time she'd cancel everything to be with him.

One summer his leave coincided with the long school holiday and they spent every day together, walking on the beach, talking, dining out. One evening they were sitting in an intimate little Italian restaurant lit only with candles when he became unusually quiet. By the time coffee was served they'd fallen into silence and she knew he was going to tell her he was about to sail again.

Panic threatened to engulf her. She wouldn't see him for months, if ever again. He never committed himself.

She was struggling to keep tears at bay when he reached across the table and took her hand, his deep dark eyes full of passion, his voice little above a whisper. 'Sarah, when I come home next leave, will you marry me?'

All the emotion she'd tried to hold in check flooded through her and her eyes welled up. She couldn't answer for the tightness in her throat, but he knew, and his eyes began to smile and his grip on her hand tightened.

Her parents were delighted, though her mother did have some reservations. 'Are you sure, dear?' she'd asked Sarah. 'You hardly know him and he is a lot older than you.'

'Only ten years, Mum. Anyway, I don't think it matters if you love each other.'

Her mum had hugged her and said of course not.

'He's a man you can trust and that's

what counts,' her dad had said.

With his long voyages and her teaching, it was another two years before they married. After the wedding they moved into Max's apartment and Sarah was happy to go along with his wishes for the time being. But she had been shocked when he suggested she give up her teaching job.

'Sarah, when will we ever see each other if I'm away at sea for months on end and when I come home you're up to your eyes in schoolwork?'

'You should be glad he wants to look after you,' her mum had said. 'I never worked after I married your dad.'

But her mum had children to care for. It was what Sarah wanted above everything and had always assumed Max would, too. But when she'd broached the subject he'd been horrified.

'Sarah, I'm thirty-six next week. I thought you knew how I felt about children.'

She'd tried to reason with him but he

would have none of it. The subject was closed.

When her sister had a baby a few months ago it came up again.

'If we have children you'll never be able to come away with me,' he'd reasoned.

'But you never want me to, anyway.'

His face had tightened with irritation so she'd let the subject drop. But during the lonely months while he was away on his next trip the ache inside her persisted.

And now here she was on board and with him. She should be full of happiness. But it wasn't how she'd expected it to be. Max wasn't the same. His mind was always elsewhere. What Geoffrey had said was probably right. The ship was a huge responsibility. But what did that leave her with in the future? Either she came on every voyage with him and felt as she did now, shut out and distant, or stayed at home ticking days off the calendar.

Shelly came up the ladder and waved

to her. She was wearing very short shorts and a skimpy top. Sarah was about to go over to her when Sebastian appeared and stood a few feet away, puffing slowly on a small cigar and eyeing Shelly up and down with interest.

Shelly glanced at him and quickly turned away. After spreading a towel on her lounger, she settled herself with a book. Sebastian sauntered over and stood looking down at her. She looked over the top of her book and said something. He answered and continued to stare at her.

Sarah felt something was wrong. Shelly seemed cross with whatever had passed between them. Shelly got up, gathered everything together and strode off back into the accommodation. Sebastian was left watching after her, a smirk on his face. Then he wandered off, still puffing at his cigar.

Sarah was puzzled. Shelly wasn't the moody type. Sebastian must have said something that had really upset her.

She got up, pulled a beach wrap over her bikini and set off round the deck.

*   *   *

Midday on Saturdays, everyone who could gathered in the officer's lounge for an informal lunch. There was a small, intimate alcove round the bar, with an arch leading through to the larger part of the room where small tables and easy chairs lined one wall, a television set and darts board took up the far end, and along the other side was a long, low unit which housed a record player and a cupboard for games. The food was laid out on this unit.

The ship was nearing the Suez Canal and everyone was talking about it.

'You won't have been through the canal, will you?' George asked Malcolm.

'No, Nasser closed it before I had a chance. I believe it's a bit tricky. No room for ships to pass. Still, at least we're in the first convoy southbound.'

'You'll be okay. Pilot takes over as soon as we arrive at Port Said,' George said.

Malcolm grunted. 'Can you see Max letting anyone take over his ship? He'll be up on that bridge keeping an eye on him.'

Maggie was walking away from the bar with a gin and tonic when Jess went up to her.

'Can we eat now, Mummy?'

'Yes, if you must,' Maggie said testily.

'Then will you play draughts with me?'

'Not now,' Maggie snapped. 'Maybe later. Give me a bit of peace, will you?'

The eager little face crumpled. 'You always say that. But you never do play with me.'

Maggie ignored her and Jess went to help herself to food, slowly working her way along the various dishes of cold meats and salads, cheese, rolls and fruit. Sarah took her drink from the bar and went to join Geoffrey. He smiled at her as she sat down beside him. 'No Max?'

'He'll be down soon. You know Max. Always checking up on something. You'd think he ran the ship single-handed.'

Geoffrey nodded. 'I'll be exactly the same when I get my command.'

'You get on well with Max, don't you?'

'I respect him. He's one of the best masters I've sailed with.'

Sarah felt a glow of pride.

'Jess is a pretty little girl, isn't she?' Geoffrey said. 'That lovely blonde hair and blue eyes.'

'She's got a sweet nature, too. Unlike her mother.'

Geoffrey laughed. 'You're right there.'

'Would you bring your children on a voyage, Geoffrey?' Sarah asked.

'I don't think Louise would be keen.' Geoffrey looked uneasy and took a drink of his beer and Sarah felt there was more to it.

George pulled up a chair to join them. 'You're looking very attractive today, my dear. Blue suits you.'

Geoffrey nudged George. 'Watch it now or you'll have Max after you.'

George looked round furtively. 'He's not here, is he?' He winked at Sarah.

Max came striding into the lounge. Jess went up to him and pulled at his sleeve. Sarah jumped up and quickly took her hand, guiding her towards the games cupboard. She knew how quickly Max could become irritated when children pestered him, especially when he was expecting a sociable chat at the bar.

Jess was easily diverted and scrambled amongst the boxes, found the one she wanted and scampered back to the table where she began to set up the draughts board next to Geoffrey.

Maggie got up and walked over to where Max was helping himself to food. He was a good head taller than Maggie and Sarah couldn't help thinking what a handsome man he was — far too arrogant, but obviously well respected.

Maggie nudged him playfully and Sarah watched with amusement. 'Now, not too much potato salad. Fattening, you know,' Maggie said to him. Her low-cut dress stretched across her bust and she had obviously had a gin and tonic too many.

Max stared down at her. 'Is that so, Mrs Grove? Well, well, you've been eating extra helpings then, haven't you?'

His voice resonated through the bar and Sarah cringed. He was in one of his playful moods, which meant everything was going well on board. But she wasn't sure Maggie would take it that way. She was sensitive about her weight and Sarah hoped she wasn't going to cause a scene.

Maggie's face lost its smile and she continued a little unsteadily along the spread of food but took very little.

Max was watching her, and then he burst into a hearty laugh. 'Good gracious, woman, have I put you off your food?'

Maggie gave him a cold look. Sarah tried to keep Jess absorbed in the game but she was looking with interest at her mother and giggling. Sarah shushed her. Max wandered over to the bar to talk to Kevin, and Maggie brought her plate and sat down quietly beside George.

'Same again?' Geoffrey asked as he gathered up the empty glasses.

'Yes, I will,' Maggie said, her face set hard.

'Are you enjoying the voyage?' George asked her in his usual jovial way.

'It's a change,' she said without looking up.

'You haven't done one for a while, have you?' George persisted.

'Not for a few years.'

'You'll have noticed a lot of changes since then.'

'The ships are bigger.'

'Certainly.' George nodded. 'The new container ships are huge.' He shook his head and sighed. 'Give me one like this any day: portholes and teak decks; lots of general cargo down in the holds instead of rows of neatly piled containers. At least you don't need a bike to get from one end to the other.'

Geoffrey put a drink each in front of

Maggie and Sarah, then sat down again.

'Attitudes are still the same, though,' Maggie said. She plonked her plate of uneaten food on the table, picked up the drink and told Jess to come with her. Jess didn't argue.

'What was all that about?' George asked.

Geoffrey shook his head. 'Usual story.'

George meandered over to the bar and stood chatting to Max. Sarah raised a questioning eyebrow to Geoffrey. He shook his head. 'Jealousy. You often find it with wives on ships.'

'What's she jealous of?'

He shrugged and took a slug at his beer, then put his glass down and looked at Sarah. 'You get treated differently. She doesn't like it.'

'I don't want to be.'

'It's the way it works on a ship. Rank counts. Captain's wife demands more respect than a chief steward's. At least that's how she feels.'

'It's not right though, is it? I can see she has a point. But I think Max was only teasing her. He didn't mean any harm.'

'Don't worry about it. It's not your problem. She'll get over it and live to rule another day.'

'She does try to organise the ship, doesn't she, with all the darts tournaments and deciding which films we show.'

He smiled. 'It does get a bit wearing. But we mostly take it in our stride. It gives her something to do.'

Max and George joined them. 'Well, it's good to be going the short route this time,' George was saying to Max. 'Let's hope there's no more trouble.'

Max picked up his beer. 'I don't think we need to worry.'

Sarah knew he did worry, not having navigated the canal since he was a junior officer. And although they would have a pilot all the way, Max would still be responsible. Soon they were all dispersing, so Sarah folded the draughts board and put it back in the box and went with Max back up to their room.

4

Too Close for Comfort

Next morning all hands were needed on deck before entering the canal, so Sarah thought she would relax in the room for a while and catch up with her diary until they were underway.

Jess found her on her way up from breakfast. 'Will you come out on deck, Sarah? I want to see Egypt.'

'I don't think there's much to see yet. Where's Mummy?'

'She's lying down. I think she's got one of her headaches.'

'Well, you be a good girl and look after Mummy and I'll see you later, once we're in the canal.'

Jess skipped ahead down the alleyway to her own room and Sarah continued up the stairs.

Max had given the order for the men

to change into whites, the tropical uniform worn in hot climates. Sarah had never seen him dressed in this uniform before, the stiff white shirt with epaulettes, knee-length white shorts and socks and buckskin shoes. It showed off his toned muscles and tanned skin, and she felt the familiar surge of excitement at seeing how handsome he looked.

He breakfasted early and went straight up onto the bridge where he intended to stay for the whole transit of the Suez Canal. Sarah eventually changed into a pair of shorts and sun top, found her sunglasses and camera and was going out of the room when she bumped into Joe. 'What are you doing around at this time? Not coffee time yet, is it?'

'No. I came to tell you we're having a party tonight. Once we're through the canal. It's down in the crew mess. We thought you might like to come. Just for a drink, like. It's Fred's birthday. You know, Fred the cook.'

'I'd love to, Joe. I'll tell Max.'

Joe looked pleased, then hesitated. 'Do you think he'll come?'

'I expect so. Unless he's tired after being on the bridge all day. I'll try and persuade him. We want to give the cook a good birthday, don't we? It's hard enough being away from your family on these special occasions. I'll come anyway.'

'Nancy and Shelly will be there. You'll enjoy it.'

Sarah went out on deck feeling light-hearted at the prospect of a little social gathering. She saw Maggie standing holding onto the rail, staring at the bank as they moved slowly along the canal, and walked over to her. 'Are you all right, Maggie?'

Maggie stared back without speaking.

'You seemed a bit put out in the bar at lunchtime yesterday.'

She turned on Sarah. 'If your husband thinks he can speak to me like that then he's mistaken.'

'I'm sure he didn't mean anything,

Maggie. Everyone gets a bit of a ribbing at times, especially in the bar at lunchtime when they've had a few drinks.'

Maggie looked her straight in the eye and shook her head. 'You think so, do you? Well, we'll see about that.'

She walked away, leaving Sarah wondering whether she should have a word with Max. But Maggie had asked for it. It was only a bit of fun. Maggie just couldn't take it. Well, she couldn't keep humouring her. They would have to sort it out between them.

She pulled a deckchair close to the rail for a good view of the canal bank as they moved slowly along. There was great activity, widening and digging, the highly sophisticated machinery seeming sadly at odds with the primitive way of life of the farming communities. In the distance she spotted a mosque, its minarets outlined against the sky, standing solitary, surrounded by miles of hot, dry sand. Who did it serve? How many miles did the people have to tramp to heed its call? All along the banks were the remains of bombed-out buildings, abandoned tanks, carnage. The war had taken a huge toll.

She tried to imagine the men stranded there for eight years. The Yellow Fleet, fourteen ships blockaded in by Nasser, so named due to all the sand that accumulated on them from the desert. She'd heard how they'd formed their own little community and set up social events. Max could so easily have been trapped there himself. He'd told her he'd only missed it by a few days.

The sun burnt into her skin and she shifted the chair into the shade of one of the lifeboats. Hard to imagine how cold it would be at home now. There was no breeze at all, just hot, humid air. She knocked a fly from her arm and it clung to her face; the beastly thing would not be diverted.

All along the lower deck were stalls selling leather goods. The Egyptians had scrambled up the gangway as soon as they'd reached Port Said, lugging great cases of goods. They would stay until Suez, then wait for a northbound convoy to sail back. She'd been pestered until she bought a wallet with a camel embossed on it and then they'd given up and left her alone.

Jess came running over to her. 'Are you going to the party tonight?'

'Yes, of course. I love parties, don't you?' Sarah said.

Jess pulled a face. 'I bet Mummy won't go. And she probably won't let me go, either. I heard her telling Daddy that the crew mess was no place for a child.'

'That's a shame.' Sarah found this segregation of crew from officers difficult to understand. They were all doing a job on board, so why couldn't they all mix together socially? But protocol on ships was different and she had to accept it.

'I want to go. I bet Daddy goes. They're having a row about it now. That's why I came out. Mummy's shouting at Daddy. She's always shouting at him.'

Sarah's heart went out to the little girl.

Jess's face brightened as she saw Geoffrey come bounding up the steps. Sarah couldn't help staring at his tanned skin against the starched whiteness of the tropical uniform, and the golden hairs on his arms glistening in the sunlight. There really was something about a man in uniform.

'Hi, gang,' he said cheerfully.

Jess ran to him and pulled at his hand.

'Not sleeping this afternoon?' Sarah asked.

He laughed. 'No chance. Not today. Every time I get my head down somebody wants something. We'll be anchoring in the Great Bitter Lake soon while the northbound convoy comes through. I might get a break then.'

He stood behind Jess and pointed to the sand dunes in the distance. 'Look, can you see the camels? Six of them.

See the men riding on them?'

Jess followed his finger and screwed up her eyes. Sarah strained to see them, too.

'Wait a minute. I'll get my binoculars.' He bounded up the ladder three steps at a time and came down again with the binoculars dangling from his shoulder. He put them to Jess's eyes. After searching for a while she shrieked, 'Oh, oh, yes, I see them.' She handed the binoculars to Sarah. Geoffrey stood behind her, put an arm on her shoulder and pointed again to where she should be looking.

She found the camels, and she was also deeply aware of Geoffrey's closeness, the pressure of his hand on her shoulder, the warmth of his body at her back, and the spicy freshness of his aftershave. She wanted this moment to last, so she kept the binoculars to her eyes long after the camels had disappeared behind a sand dune.

Jess saw Nancy appear on deck and went running over to her. She grabbed her hand and pulled her to the rail and pointed. Nancy's long skirt spread out on the deck as she crouched to see what Jess was looking at. Sarah watched in surprise. Geoffrey was right. Nancy was pretty when she smiled. And she seemed happy to be with Jess.

* * *

Max stared ahead from the bridge window. He'd be glad when they were through the Suez Canal. The pilot was competent, he knew, but the final responsibility lay with him. The whole damned ship was his responsibility and he wished Sarah could understand that.

He banged his fists down on the wooden ledge in front of him, causing eyes to turn, but he didn't care. What was wrong with him? It had been his life for twenty-odd years and he knew ships better than anything else. Why was he suddenly so unsettled? He had Sarah here with him. He didn't have to sit in his lonely cabin night after night longing for her as he had done last trip. She seemed happy on the whole and didn't interfere like some wives he'd come across on ships, not like that awful Maggie. And she didn't hang around him endlessly as Nancy did with Malcolm. But she did want more of him than he could give and he didn't know how to deal with it.

He marched out onto the wing of the bridge and saw Jess skipping with an old piece of rope. It wasn't often children appealed to him but this one had something about her. Sarah spent a lot of time with the child, too.

Again his mind became troubled and a stab of guilt caught him unawares. He must talk to Sarah. She had a right to know why he felt the way he did about having children. A cold shiver ran through him. His heart ached to give her what she most wanted but he just couldn't take that risk.

Jess was an exceptional child. Her mother was a good-looking woman with plenty of man appeal. Pity help the man who tangled with her, though. Poor old Kevin. What would he do this time when they got to Bangkok? The thought brought a smile to his lips.

He walked through the chartroom and looked down onto the deck below. Geoffrey had his arm round Sarah as she peered through the binoculars into the distance. His smile quickly faded and he felt a sudden cold fear. Geoffrey took his arm from her as she handed the binoculars back, smiling up at him in a way which tore at Max's heart. They were laughing about something now and Jess was dancing round excitedly. Max felt an intense jealousy.

For the next few hours he was impatient to get down off the bridge. His legs ached from standing all day and he wanted a shower and a drink. And he wanted to be with Sarah. He wanted to shut his door and sit and talk to her. He would try to tell her some of the things he felt.

* * *

It was well after eight before they cleared Suez. The lights were already on in the streets and Max could see people moving about and a stream of traffic in the main road. When he finally got down to his room the sight of Sarah curled up in the big easy chair with her book cheered him. She looked up and smiled, her dark hair shining. She was wearing his favourite red dress and the seductive fragrance that always worked its magic on him.

She looked up with a bright smile. 'We've been invited down to the crew bar tonight. They're having a party for Fred's birthday.'

He stared at her with complete incomprehension.

'We will join them, won't we?' she asked eagerly.

He frowned. 'Sarah, I'm worn out.'

'Oh, yes. I'm sorry.' There was disappointment in her voice. 'Maybe later on. Couldn't we just go down for one drink? I don't want us to seem unsociable.'

He had looked forward to this

71

evening. After a day full of tension he wanted these few hours alone with Sarah. And now she had these mad notions about parties.

'Sarah, we don't have to be sociable. I am master on this vessel and I do not have to go hob-nobbing with my crew. If they want a party they can have it, so long as they do their job and don't cause a disturbance. Now, all I want is a quiet drink and an early night.'

Sarah frowned. 'I'll go then,' she said defiantly.

Max tensed. 'Neither of us is going down and that is final. They'll be drinking themselves silly and the language will be choice. You've never been down to the crew mess. It's not the same as the officers' lounge. You don't know what it's like when they get going.'

Sarah's eyes blazed. 'They're nice people, friendly and kind.'

'How do you know?' he snapped.

She jumped up and faced him. 'Because I talk to them. There's nothing wrong with that is there?'

He sighed.

'If you want to shut yourself away up here, don't expect me to stay with you,' she told him. 'I like people and I need friends and . . . '

Max watched as she rushed from the room into the bathroom, locking the door. What could he do? He could not go down there and drink and joke with these men. Not for Sarah, not for anyone. She was making his position impossible. He poured himself a large Scotch and sank into the swivel chair at his desk. He was too worn out to argue. Sarah must do as she pleased.

* * *

Geoffrey caught up with her later when she was taking a stroll round the deck in the cool night air. 'Thought you'd be at the party. Should be well underway by now. They always make an effort for a birthday.'

'Max won't go. He says he's tired.'

'You go, then. You'll enjoy it. They'd

73

make you very welcome. I'll be along myself shortly when I've done my rounds.'

'I don't know. It doesn't seem right to go without him. They'll all wonder where he is.'

'They'll know he's had a long day. Come on, Sarah. Cheer up.' He paused. 'I tell you what. I'll promise Max I'll take special care of you if he lets you go. How about that?'

She smiled and shook her head, knowing he would never dare.

★ ★ ★

They sat in the room, both with a book but neither reading. Max picked up his drink and Sarah glanced at him. He didn't return her look but continued to stare obstinately at the glass. She looked at her watch. Ten thirty. The party would be in full swing now, and again a surge of anger and annoyance welled up in her. Everyone but the watch-keepers would be there. She fidgeted with her bracelet, swirling it round and round on her wrist. She would go down. Why shouldn't she?

But somehow her legs wouldn't let her get off the settee. Her voice wouldn't say the words. She was reluctant to arouse his anger again. The words in her book blurred into black shapes on a white page. Geoffrey would be there. It couldn't be that rough or he wouldn't have suggested she go. She turned the page for effect. If only Max would relax and not be so pompous. They could both go to the party just for a while and it would do Max good to socialise a bit.

She looked round the room. She'd liked the room when she first saw it but now she knew every detail so well. The picture of palm trees on a sandy beach. That curtain that didn't hang quite right. The stark white light from the desk lamp Max focused on his book when he was reading. They should be enjoying this time together instead of sitting like this. If only he would bend a little.

There was a knock at the door.

'Yes?' Max barked.

Geoffrey popped his head round. 'Excuse me, sir. Would you and Sarah like to join us for a drink? We're celebrating Fred's birthday.'

Max peered over his glass at Geoffrey. 'No, I think not. But send him our good wishes.'

Sarah jumped up from the settee. 'I'd like to go.' She didn't look at Max but could feel his eyes on her.

'Good. I know your presence will be much appreciated. A little female company always helps things along.'

Sarah felt as if she was walking a tight-rope and before she could fall she quickly made for the door and, turning only briefly before she went through it, said to Max, 'I won't stay long.'

When she was down the first flight of stairs and along the alleyway Sarah stopped and leant against the bulkhead, her heart beating wildly. She looked up at Geoffrey and pulled a face. 'I don't know how I'm going to face him when I get back, but I'm going to enjoy this evening.'

He was standing very close to her, his face just above hers. The slightest shadow touched his eyes. Then he gave her a conspiratorial smile. 'Told you I'd fix it.'

5

Challenging Times for Sarah

As they made their way along the decks, Sarah stopped. The sky above them was a deep, dark velvet, pierced with a million diamonds, a wisp of moon reflecting in the still, deep water, the air warm and gentle after the heat of the day as the ship moved smoothly through the water. She was acutely aware of Geoffrey standing behind her and felt an all-consuming need for him to enfold her in his arms and make the hurt and loneliness go away. When she turned, their eyes met and time stood still. She was aware only of that moment. In the moonlight she could see the same longing in his. Then he put an arm round her waist. 'Come on, party girl.' The moment had passed.

The crew mess was lit with small

lamps giving it a warm glow and the noise of chatter and laughter met them as they walked in through the door. Joe was changing the tape in the player. He turned and smiled as he felt Jess pulling at his sleeve.

'Hello, little one. You're up late tonight.'

Geoffrey left Sarah talking to Jess and went to get them a drink. The sound of Earth, Wind and Fire came belting out of the speakers so that she could hardly hear what Jess was saying, but was glad of the distraction as gradually she began to bring her feelings under control.

She stood sipping the wine Geoffrey handed to her and he leant on the bar smiling as she swayed to the music. The ship was now sailing smoothly on course for the Indian Ocean and a long stretch at sea, so the men could relax and enjoy a drink after a tiring day traversing the canal.

'Mummy doesn't know I'm here.' Jess hunched her shoulders and giggled.

'She's in bed with a headache. I couldn't sleep so Daddy said I could come down for a while. She'd go absolutely spare if she knew I was here!'

Joe took Jess's hands and began to jig round to the music in the small space that had been cleared in the middle of the room, and Sarah joined in. Then Jess went off to the bar to talk to her dad.

'She's a great kid,' Joe said to Sarah as they stood and watched her.

'You really like children, don't you, Joe? You'll make a great dad.'

He grinned. 'Can't wait. Some people don't know when they're lucky.'

Sarah thought how true that was.

'Look at her father, already had a skinful. And her mother's not much better.' He shook his head and ambled off towards the bar.

Geoffrey came over to where Sarah was standing. 'What's wrong with Joe?'

'He's worried about Jess.'

He shrugged. 'Everyone looks out for her and she seems pretty sensible.'

'Maggie does try,' Sarah said.

'Yes, she has her faults but she does care for Jess,' Geoffrey agreed. 'It's Kevin I feel sorry for. Come on, let's go and talk to him.'

They wandered over to the bar but Kevin was now in conversation with Jack, one of the seamen Sarah had seen on deck.

Kevin raised a glass to her and said how pleased he was she'd come. 'Not managed to bring the captain?'

Sarah explained that he was worn out after being up on the bridge all day.

'Well, it's very nice to have you here.'

Jack turned to Kevin. 'Where's your young lady then, Kev?'

'She wouldn't come to a do like this.'

'Well, you've got a nice warm bed to go back to,' Jack said, nudging his arm and spilling his whisky onto the bar.

Kevin looked hard at him. 'You think so, do you?' He stared morosely into his glass. 'She's all right, is Maggie. I mean she puts up with me, doesn't she, and I'm no great shakes.'

'Och, man. I canna see why a good looking woman like her would ever marry a drunken sod like you.'

'I know,' Kevin said morbidly. 'Mind, I wasn't a drunkard then. But still, she could've done better.' He picked up his whisky and swallowed the lot. 'Cheers,' he said, holding up the empty glass.

'What you gonna do in Bangkok, then?' Jack said with a smirk. 'You'll have to behave this time, won't you, mate?'

Kevin frowned into his glass and grunted.

The tall, dark figure standing at the end of the bar was quietly watching and listening. He puffed at a large black cigar and blew a cloud of smoke into the air. Then he shook his head in amusement. Sarah looked away. Whatever he was up to was bound to be bad. She didn't trust Sebastian.

Geoffrey took Sarah's arm and pulled her to one side away from the bar. 'I didn't realise quite how much they'd had to drink. Once they've had a skinful they can get pretty crude. And I did promise to look after you.'

Sarah smiled. 'I think I can cope. I'm sure they don't mean any harm.'

They stood in quiet companionship watching Jess chattering with Shelly, who looked stunning in a halter-neck catsuit in an exotic tropical print. Her hair hung round her shoulders in a profusion of auburn curls and her face was glowing with happiness.

'Shelly's a nice kid,' Geoffrey said, following Sarah's gaze. 'And good at her job.'

'It must be strange working with all you men. Is she coping all right?'

He looked doubtful. 'I'm not sure. There does seem to be a problem with Nancy.'

Sarah frowned. 'What do you mean? I can't imagine Nancy causing a problem. She never bothers with anyone except Malcolm.'

'Shelly's on watch with him quite a lot. I don't think Nancy likes it.'

'You think she doesn't trust him?'

He shook his head slowly. 'It's not good having one girl on a ship like this. Bound to cause trouble. A cargo ship's a strange environment. Men cooped up for months on end.'

Sarah stared at him. 'You don't think I should be here, then?'

'Of course you should.' And she was rewarded by one of his lovely smiles.

'But you wouldn't bring your wife.' She couldn't help feeling a little hurt.

'Louise wouldn't come. Kids and all that.' The smile vanished as he took her arm and they went to the side of the room and sat at one of the tables.

Sarah couldn't see Nancy anywhere and assumed she wouldn't want to come to a gathering like this without Malcolm.

Joe and Jess came over. 'We're selling draw tickets,' Jess said excitedly. 'There's an enormous teddy for a prize. You've got to buy one, Sarah.'

Joe took her money while Jess carefully tore out the tickets. Geoffrey bought some and seemed restored to his usual good humour. He was right, though: a ship like this was a strange environment. Max was probably right, too, and she should have stayed with him tonight. Yet she felt alive down here with the music and laughter. And with Geoffrey beside her. The thought gave her a jolt. She shouldn't be thinking this way. She'd finish this drink and get back to Max.

The lights dimmed and she leant back and closed her eyes as the velvet tones of Barry Manilow singing 'I Write the Songs' floated through the room. Some of the men were getting up and leaving. A few were in conversation round the bar and Shelly and Ben were swaying together in the middle of the room. Music and laughter floated over her as the wine took hold.

Geoffrey touched her arm and shook her out of her thoughts. 'Let's dance.'

She staggered slightly as she tried to get up and he steadied her, then took her in his arms. Her head rested on his shoulder. The skin of his cheek was soft and his hair touched her temple gently.

She felt safe in his arms, safe and happy. He had said he would look after her and she knew he would. 'Hold Me Close' drifted through the loudspeakers and she relaxed against him as he drew her closer, her conscience smothered in a contented blur.

* * *

Maggie turned restlessly in her bed. Her head didn't feel so bad now. She'd had a lot of these heads lately. And a lot of sympathy she got from Kevin. He'd be out of his mind in that bar by now if she knew anything. The very idea of him wanting to take her and Jess down there; to expose them to all that swearing and drinking. The uncomfortable thought that Sarah might be there enjoying herself was quickly pushed out of her mind.

She reached for the light switch and looked at the clock. Midnight. She was thirsty and went across the room to the wash basin to get a glass of water, glancing automatically at the mattress they put up at night for Jess. She gasped. The bed was empty. The child was at that party. She'd murder Kevin.

She struggled into a loose caftan which was hanging over a chair, not caring that her hair was in disarray, and rushed from the room and down the alleyway.

* * *

Sarah knew she shouldn't be feeling this way. If Max had come down here with her it would have been different. They would have had a couple of drinks and a chat then gone back up to the room. Geoffrey was married. And so was she. And they were dancing together and the whole ship could see them. All these thoughts went through the fuzziness of her mind.

Art Garfunkel was crooning 'I Only Have Eyes for You' and Geoffrey pulled away slightly and as their eyes met she knew it had gone too far.

She broke away from him but he grabbed her arm as she tried to walk away. 'What's up?'

'We shouldn't be dancing like this. I'd better get back. It's very late.'

He let go. 'I'll walk you back.'

She gave a feeble laugh. 'No need. I'm hardly likely to come to harm on a ship. I promise I won't throw myself overboard.'

He put his arm round her shoulder and guided her towards the door. The air was warm and humid, the sea a black sheet, reflecting only a silver strip of moonlight. As they lingered on the tiny space of deck, reluctant to leave something so beautiful, their fingers touched and Sarah looked up into his face, dark in the moonlight, and saw a longing to match her own. He was going to kiss her and she wanted him to. His lips came slowly towards hers and she closed her eyes in expectation.

But he straightened and walked over to the rail and was staring out over the sea. She went to stand beside him.

'We can't, Sarah. You know we can't.' His voice was tight with passion as he turned to look at her, his face distraught. 'I'm sorry.'

They walked silently back across the deck and, standing beside the door, they saw Maggie. She'd seen them together. She'd seen how close they'd been to kissing. She moved aside to let them through, her eyes following them until the door closed.

*   *   *

Maggie took in the scene in the mess. Kevin was propping up the bar. A group were singing bawdy songs. Ben and Shelly were holding each other up in the middle of the floor. Then she saw Jess curled up on Joe's knee, his arm round her, his chin resting on her head with his eyes closed.

She flew at him and dragged the dazed child from him roughly and, without a word, made her way out of the room. Joe jumped up in alarm and raced after her, catching her just as she reached the door. 'I was going to bring her up in a minute.'

Maggie turned on him. 'She should never have been here in the first place.' Then she turned towards the bar. 'Look at her father. Can't even stand up. What sort of a place is this to bring a child?'

Joe stood speechless. The whole room was silenced, watching the scene. Jess was whimpering and clinging to Maggie, still half asleep, not knowing what all the shouting was about. Kevin watched Maggie drag her out of the room and shook his head.

★   ★   ★

Sarah woke late next morning. Her head ached and she didn't feel like coping with the problems stretching before her. Max had been asleep when she'd crept into bed last night. She'd lain awake for hours reliving the feel of Geoffrey's arms around her, how alive she had felt dancing with Jess, the noise, the music, the laughter. Then coming back to this quiet room with Max asleep.

This morning reality forced itself upon her. She had to face Max. But worse, she had to face Geoffrey. Until last night they had shared a happy friendship and that was all. But last night had been different. What had seemed so right and beautiful under the stars now filled her with shame. And Maggie had seen them together. Maggie disliked her and would enjoy making trouble.

Sarah closed her eyes. If only she could escape once more in sleep. If only she could spend the whole day in bed and not have to face any of them. But if she did, there would still be tomorrow. She had to live with all these people for the rest of the voyage. And she had to live with Max for ever, listening to symphony concerts on the radio, a glass of whisky and a book in the evening, then long months alone when he went off on his ship again. She wanted more from life. She wanted fun and friends and laughter. And more than anything, she yearned for that one thing she would never have.

She pulled herself up short. What was she thinking? Max wasn't always like this. At home he was fun. He took her out to lovely restaurants and wined and dined her. They gave dinner parties for friends. They talked and laughed and made love. She was happy with Max. When he was home on leave it was the happiest time of her life. She hated it when he went away. She loved him. He was her husband. He was a good man and he adored her, she knew. So what was she thinking? It was being on this ship with so little to do whilst he was always busy. She should be more understanding. He had warned her. She should have listened. If only she had someone to talk to. Max never gave her his full attention. They hardly ever had time alone. She was lonely. She needed a friend. Her heart gave a painful twist. Maggie hated her. Nancy was too wrapped up in Malcolm. She just had Geoffrey.

There was no sign of Max, which gave her a bit more time to sort out her troubled mind. She had a shower and dressed. She wanted coffee badly. Max got annoyed if she went down to the galley and made her own. She wouldn't have done that this morning anyway. She didn't want to see anyone.

If she rang down now Joe would bring coffee up. She wouldn't mind seeing Joe. He wouldn't judge her and she might feel better if she talked to someone. Suddenly she wanted to see Joe as much as she wanted the coffee.

But when Joe brought the coffee he seemed quieter, his face more gaunt.

'What's up, Joe?'

He looked at her with troubled eyes. 'I don't like what happened last night,' he said flatly.

Sarah took the tray from him. 'What happened?'

Joe stared at his big, black shoes. 'All I did was look after her. Her father was drunk and I didn't know what to do.' He looked at Sarah for reassurance. 'She was tired and she fell asleep on my knee. And then her mother came in and started shouting at me.'

Sarah didn't know what to say so put a hand on his arm.

Max paced into the room at that moment. He stood and stared at them. Sarah quickly withdrew her hand. Joe looked at Max then turned and walked out of the room without a word.

Sarah waited. But Max said nothing. He poured the coffee, sat at his desk, muttered something about the mate and cargo declarations and began stabbing at his typewriter.

When he left the room again Sarah went out on deck. She couldn't hide away all day. She had to spend the next few months on the ship with all these people so she might as well get it over with.

As she pounded the deck on her usual morning walk, she heard Jess, then saw Geoffrey fixing a swing up for her behind one of the hatches. Jess was excited and wanting to get on it but Geoffrey insisted on testing it first. He swung a few times and the ropes groaned under his weight. Then he saw Sarah.

Jess saw her, too. 'Sarah, come and have a go on my swing,' she shrieked.

Sarah shrugged. She wasn't sure her voice would make the right sounds.

'Come on, Sarah,' Geoffrey encouraged. 'Let's see if your swinging is as good as your skipping.'

Sarah approached the swing cautiously, sat on the seat and pushed off with her foot. Geoffrey came up behind and gave a gentle push. Her heart was beating wildly and she had difficulty holding her hand steady on the ropes. As he pulled her back to give another push, he held the swing so he could whisper in her ear. 'No harm done. Can we forget it happened?'

She nodded and breathed again. He'd made it all right. Her embarrassment faded. She could face him now. She let the swing go to and fro. Jess watched, impatient to be on it. Geoffrey gave her one hard push with a whoop of laughter then went on his way back up the deck. Her heart was light. She jumped off the swing and let Jess take over.

* * *

The lounge was full when Sarah and Max went down for a drink before lunch. Malcolm smiled at her then continued his conversation with Shelly. Maggie was sitting in a corner letting forth to George. She briefly acknowledged Sarah as she passed her table but there was no indication that she recalled last night. It seemed as if it had never happened. Nobody treated her any differently. Max seemed like his usual self. Sarah began to feel a little safer. Maybe it would all pass over. All she had to do now was keep her mind on Max and enjoy the voyage. Everyone seemed in good spirits and the bar was noisy with talk and laughter as usual.

★ ★ ★

As the ship made its way across the Indian Ocean the social life on board really started to build up. The men had settled in and got to know each other and a sense of comradeship began to develop.

Max came out on deck with a gin and tonic for Sarah late one afternoon as she sat watching the sun slowly sink towards the horizon.

He pointed out to sea. 'Look over there. Can you see them?'

She jumped up and saw, to her delight, the tail fins of leaping dolphins. He stood behind her at the rail watching the show as the sun settled in a great ball of fire, turning the sea into molten gold.

'They're showing a film in the lounge tomorrow evening after dinner. Do you fancy a bit of light entertainment?'

Of course she did. Especially if it was something Max was going to enjoy too.

'What are they showing?'

'*The Towering Inferno.* They were going to show *The Godfather* but I didn't think that was quite to your taste. I'm afraid the films they show on board are rather male-orientated.'

'Sounds fine to me. I've heard it's very good.'

They sat quietly each side of the small round table, looking out across the sea. Max reached across and took her hand. 'Are you happy, Sarah?'

She turned and looked into his eyes. 'Max, of course I am. I'm with you, aren't I?'

He squeezed her hand as they sat watching the sky turn a blazing red, then went inside, his arm around her.

6

Unrest on Board

When Sarah went down for a swim next morning she was shocked to see Nancy standing at the side of the pool fully dressed and dripping with water. Jess stood beside her in her bikini, shaking and taking deep breaths. When she saw Sarah approach, Nancy walked unsteadily towards one of the deckchairs and lowered herself into it, head bowed, wet hair straggling over her shoulders.

'Jess, what happened?' Sarah said, turning the child to face her.

Jess was sobbing between gasps. 'I nearly drowned. Nancy got me out.'

Sarah looked at Nancy. She was shaking and staring at her clenched hands in her lap, her wet skirt clinging to her legs and dripping a pool of water round the chair. 'Jess, what's wrong with Nancy?'

'She can't swim. We both nearly drowned. She got me to the side and we got out up the ladder.'

Once Sarah had made sure Jess had recovered, she went to Nancy. Nancy stiffened as Sarah sat beside her.

'Nancy, are you all right?'

Nancy nodded but didn't look up.

'Nancy, you need to go inside and get changed.'

Nancy didn't move. Jess stood watching.

Sarah didn't know what to do. She couldn't leave Nancy. She tried again. 'Nancy, you're shaking. You need to come inside.'

Nancy tried to get up but her legs buckled under her. She flopped back down again. Sarah turned back to Jess but she'd gone. She stood up and looked round anxiously. Then just as she was about to go and look for her, Maggie appeared with Jess in tow behind her.

Maggie ignored Sarah and strode over to Nancy. 'Come on, my girl, up you get,' and she yanked Nancy out of the seat. Sarah stared in amazement as Nancy detached herself from Maggie, straightened and then shakily followed her through the door.

Jess was shivering and her teeth chattered. Sarah wrapped her in a towel and hugged her.

'I thought I could swim all the way across,' Jess sobbed. 'Then I couldn't breathe. Then Nancy jumped in and got me out.'

Sarah led her to one of the deckchairs and sat beside her.

'Nancy told me she's really frightened of water. That's why she's gone all shaky. Mummy will look after her. She's good at things like that. She always knows what to do.'

Sarah had the feeling she had underestimated both these women. She made sure Jess went back to her room, then found a seat in the sun and worried that it might all have been her fault for encouraging Jess to swim. Maggie was sure to have a go at her now.

But when she saw her later that

afternoon in the lounge Maggie didn't mention it. She was studying the darts match chart she'd pinned to the wall. 'At least some of them are taking this seriously.'

Sarah looked at the list of matches Maggie had organised. 'I suppose there's plenty of time.'

'Not the point. I wanted them played before we get to Penang. Nobody will have time after that. We need to get it done while we're on this long drag at sea.'

'Did they seem enthusiastic when you suggested it?'

'Oh, that lot never do. You just have to get them organised. Wouldn't do a thing if I didn't chivvy them along. I used to do it on every ship. But this lot aren't interested. Got no go in them at all.'

'Was Nancy all right?' Sarah said.

Maggie shrugged. 'Nothing a large brandy didn't sort. Good thing she was out there. I keep telling Jess not to go in the water unless you're there with her. But she never listens. Got a mind of her own, has that one.'

Sarah breathed a sigh of relief.

* * *

When she mentioned the darts match to Max he let out a great guffaw. 'I'll give her full marks for trying. Now if you'd organised it they'd all have rallied round.'

'I'm certainly not getting involved,' Sarah said.

'You're not frightened of her, are you?' he teased.

Sarah snorted. 'I think we all are.'

* * *

Sarah was concerned for Nancy as neither she nor Malcolm had appeared in the bar or for dinner, but when she went to her room to check she was all right Nancy had barely opened the door and had made it quite clear she didn't want to be disturbed. Malcolm told Sarah that she was quite recovered and that there was no need for concern. Sarah found it all rather odd but decided that if Nancy preferred to be left alone then she should respect that.

★ ★ ★

The film that evening was shown on a roll-down screen from a noisy projector. They sat in rows on hard chairs but it was fun and Sarah enjoyed the change. After the film, she and Max stood out on deck listening to the gentle wash of the waves and watching a shoal of flying fish leaping out of the water, their translucent fins flashing rays of colour in the moonlight.

It was cooler out there and Max put an arm round her and led her along the length of the deck and up into the bow of the ship where they stood on the fo'csle. A light breeze ruffled her hair and she began to feel with Max the passion he felt for his ship as she steadily cut through the water, causing bow waves to break along her sides with a gentle murmur. He turned her to him and kissed her gently beneath the stars and her whole body relaxed into the moment. That night she felt closer to Max than she had for a long time and fell asleep in his arms.

* * *

They were nearing Sri Lanka and Max was looking forward to taking Sarah ashore. He walked out onto his deck and looked down on the swimming pool. Sarah was trying to get Jess to do the crawl, beside her all the time talking encouraging words. Jess was floundering with her arms and legs, deep concentration on her face. Max couldn't hear what was being said but he could read her body language. Sarah was so patient.

When she let go, Jess made it all the way to the side under her own steam. She gripped the edge of the pool and hoisted herself clear of the water to get her breath, then turned to Sarah, a look of sheer joy on her face. Sarah's face was a picture of happiness. They hugged and splashed back in the water, then Sarah hoisted Jess out of the pool to sit on the side and rest.

Max felt a lump in his throat. Was he depriving Sarah of something so fundamental to her happiness? He felt a pain deep within him he could hardly bear. She was a natural with children. She should have a brood of her own just like her sister. And here she was, stuck with him, and would never have any at all. Should he put his fears aside for Sarah's happiness? He didn't think he could. He would give her anything she wanted, but not that. He turned away and began to climb up to the bridge.

*   *   *

Word got round that Ben and Shelly were organising a horse-race meeting on deck. It seemed everyone had mid-voyage blues and this would cheer things up.

'Wooden horses moved along a course on the toss of a dice,' Max explained. 'Some of the crew bet quite heavily, but mostly it's an excuse for a night out on deck and a bit of fun.'

By eight o'clock the preparations were complete. A few of the men were gathering; the deck bar was open and music playing. Coloured lights hung between the derricks and lifeboats, and beyond was the gentle murmur of the sea. Ben was setting up the track which ran the length of the pool deck. Max seemed in a relaxed mood and put a bet on a horse called Pretty Lady and told Sarah it was for her.

Sarah looked up and sighed. 'The stars are so much brighter here.'

'No light pollution,' Max said.

He went off to get drinks and Sarah relaxed back in her seat, enjoying the enchantment of an evening under the stars on a calm sea in tropical warmth. Max came back with two drinks, one of which looked like a fruit salad in a very tall glass with a straw stuck in. She puffed out her cheeks and gave a snort of laughter. He handed it to her with a shake of his head. 'Kevin made it specially for you.'

Jess was happily tossing the dice, which would decide how far each horse would move. Kevin was looking on and Malcolm and Nancy were sitting talking together. Shelly was drinking from a bottle by the side of the pool. Some sailors came up from the deck below and noisily ordered drinks. Just about everyone was on deck now. Joe came round with baskets of hot chicken. The coloured lights gave a warm glow that was reflected in the swimming pool. Sarah leant back and let the magic of the evening wash over her.

Malcolm and Nancy got up to dance. Max pulled Sarah up from her deck-chair and took her in his arms. As they smooched to the sound of David Essex crooning 'Hold Me Close', Max drew her closer and she snuggled into him. She remembered dancing with Geoffrey to the same song but this time there was no guilt, just perfect contentment. This was what she had wanted the voyage to be. Time with Max. Together. It was what she always wanted.

When the music stopped, Max took her hand and they walked to the rail and gazed out into the deep, dark sea, aware only of each other and the gentle rhythm of the ship gliding through the water. Max put an arm round her shoulder. 'Nothing but sea and stars,' he murmured. 'No sound but the power of the ship ploughing ever onward.' He turned to her, his voice deep with passion. 'Can you feel it, Sarah?' She looked into his deep, dark eyes and knew he had everything he wanted at that moment, his wife at his side and the deck beneath his feet.

All too soon they were clearing away. Kevin took Jess to bed. Maggie lingered, looking a little the worse for wear. There were only a few people out on deck, talking quietly or relaxing in the cool of the evening. One of the sailors was taking the coloured lights down. They moved the bar back inside but the music still filtered through the cool night air, refreshing after the heat of the day.

'Come on, my love,' Max said. 'Let's go back in and have a nightcap.'

She looked up at him and smiled. As they made their way up she noticed Shelly standing by the rail staring out to sea. When Sarah shouted good night to her she turned but didn't reply.

'I'm just going to have a word with Shelly,' Sarah told Max.

He looked surprised but didn't object. 'Don't be long, then. I'll pour the drinks.'

She kissed him on the cheek and went over to Shelly. 'You're not looking too happy.'

Shelly turned to her. 'I'm fed up.'

'Why's that? The evening was a great success. You and Ben did a good job.'

When Shelly spoke, her voice was strained and Sarah could sense she was near to tears. 'Shelly, what is it?'

Shelly gripped the rail and stared ahead. 'It's Nancy.'

'What's she done?'

'Nothing.' There was a long pause. Sarah waited. Shelly took a deep breath. 'Whenever I speak to Malcolm she stares at me. I've tried to be friendly. I've never done anything to upset her. Why's she like that?'

Sarah sighed.

Shelly's voice began to tremble. 'And Sebastian won't leave me alone. And George keeps passing remarks. I'm fed up with it all.'

Sarah put an arm round her shoulder. 'Shelly, listen to me. Nancy's the same with me. It's just her way. Sebastian's trouble, so ignore him and I'm sure George doesn't mean any harm.'

Shelly shook her head and stared out over the sea.

Sarah squeezed her shoulder. 'I'll tell you something. Max is impressed with you. And that's saying a lot.'

Shelly turned a tear-stained face to her. 'Is he?'

Sarah smiled. 'Yes, he is. Now stop all this nonsense. Keep your head down and get on with the job and I think you'll find you leave this ship with a glowing report.'

Shelly wiped her eyes on the back of her hand. 'Thanks, Sarah.'

Sarah watched her go back inside. It was cool out on deck and so peaceful. Shelly was obviously feeling homesick. Sebastian was a nasty piece of work and this business with Nancy was unsettling her. Malcolm came ambling along checking all was well and wandered over to her. 'Just seen you talking to young Shelly.'

Sarah smiled at him. 'A bit homesick.'

He leant on the rail beside her, looking out to sea. 'First few trips are always tough. Even the boys get homesick.'

'She is getting a lot of ribbing from certain quarters.'

'Afraid she'll have to get used to that. Bound to happen.'

'Couldn't you all ease off a little? Give her a fighting chance?'

He looked shocked. 'It's not me. I have a lot of respect for her.'

'I know that, Malcolm. But you could maybe spread the word. Let it be known that it's upsetting her.'

He shrugged. 'I'll try, but I doubt it'll make any difference.'

Malcolm went on his way, whistling. He obviously didn't see any problem with Nancy. Maybe Shelly was being too sensitive and would have to toughen up if she was to survive in this environment.

Sarah was out on deck next day playing quoits with Jess when Geoffrey walked past, swinging a large brass instrument in his hand.

'Where are you going?' Jess asked him.

'I'm going up on the bridge to take sights. I do that every day at noon.'

'What's that?' Jess asked.

He swung the shiny brass instrument up in both hands and put it in front of her. 'Its called a sextant and it enables me to find the exact position of the ship by measuring the angle between the stars and the horizon.'

Jess examined it, then looked at Geoffrey. 'But it's daytime. There aren't any stars yet.'

'Oh, but there are. There is one very bright one.'

Jess stopped him and jumped up and down. 'I know what it is. It's the sun.'

'Correct.' Geoffrey smiled at her.

'But you're not supposed to look at the sun. My teacher said that when we had an eclipse thing.'

'Ah, but this instrument has special filters so that I can look at it and not hurt my eyes.'

'Gosh, that's clever,' Jess said.

'Do you want to come up on the bridge and watch me?' Geoffrey said, grinning at her. Then he looked at Sarah. 'Do you want to come up, too?'

Sarah was reluctant but couldn't refuse when confronted with Jess's excited face. After Geoffrey had lined up his sextant and taken the readings they went into the chartroom and he pointed on the chart to exactly where they were in the middle of the Indian

Ocean. He didn't touch Sarah but she was acutely aware of his closeness and had to steel herself not to show her feelings. As their eyes met she knew it was as difficult for him as it was for her. But he seemed able to cope with it so much more easily.

'It's a very important piece of equipment,' Geoffrey told Jess. 'I take stars at midnight as well. When you're fast asleep in bed.'

'Can I watch one night?' Jess asked.

'Maybe.' Again he glanced at Sarah, then quickly back at Jess. 'Now off you go. I have to make an entry in the logbook.' Their eyes met again as she took Jess's hand and turned to go.

'Can we look up about sextants in my lesson tomorrow?' Jess asked Sarah once they were back on deck.

Sarah fought to bring her mind back to what Jess was saying. 'What a good idea. I'll ask Max if he has any books about them, then perhaps you could draw one.'

When she asked Max he shook his

head. 'No need for books. I'll join you tomorrow for the lesson. I'll get my sextant out and she can draw that, then I'll answer all her questions.'

'Max, that would be wonderful. She's so keen to learn.'

He grunted. 'Good. Her mother must be doing something right, then.'

★ ★ ★

Next day when Sarah came into the room after her morning walk to give Jess her lesson, she hadn't arrived. Usually she was very prompt and keen. After waiting a while she went to look for her and eventually found her up on the bridge in the chartroom with Max. They were poring over a chart Max had laid out on the table for her to see.

'Ah, here you are. I'm afraid Jess was a little confused about the time this morning. She hadn't adjusted her watch. So I thought I'd explain why we keep putting it forward an hour.'

Jess looked up at Sarah. 'Can I stay

here and listen some more?'

'Of course. You just carry on and I'll listen too, then we can both learn.'

Max continued to explain to Jess how the time zones worked and how every time they crossed one, going east, they had to add an hour to the clocks. 'If we reached the international date line we would gain a whole day. Then we have to adjust so Monday becomes Sunday.'

Jess looked confused. 'But Sunday comes before Monday. That's the wrong way round.' She looked at him, disbelieving. 'How can that happen?'

He laughed. 'Now I have things to do, so you go back with Sarah and try to work it out.' He looked towards Sarah with a wicked grin and she frowned, but her heart was smiling.

* * *

As they neared the equator the temperature continued to rise and dusk came earlier. There were many pleasant evenings sitting with Max on the quarterdeck, just the two of them, drinking gin and tonics as the ship glided through the water.

It was a hot day with a clear blue sky, the water still and peaceful, when they anchored off Penang, waiting for a berth. There were plans to take two of the lifeboats and find a quiet beach for a picnic as the ship was idle for a day.

'Why won't you come?' Sarah asked Max when she came in from her morning swim.

'Not my sort of thing. All that sand and blazing hot sun. No, I shall be quite content on board with my book.'

She felt a stab of hurt that he would prefer his book to taking her ashore. There seemed no reason for him to stay on board as Malcolm was doing anchor watch. It almost seemed he wanted her out of the way so he could have a bit of peace. But she swallowed the hurt and changed into a sundress and sandals, determined to enjoy the outing with the others.

'Couldn't Malcolm come as well if

you're staying on board?' she asked Max.

He shook his head. 'This isn't a cruise ship. My officers are paid to do a job.'

She shrugged and sighed. She had hoped Geoffrey would be the one to stay on board and do anchor watch. Since the party he had been pleasant and friendly towards her but she was always aware of him whenever he was near and felt a whole day on the beach was going to be difficult.

As they assembled on deck Sarah tried to keep as far from Maggie as possible in the hope she wouldn't end up in the same lifeboat. They'd got on better lately but she still didn't enjoy her company.

Kevin staggered up from the galley with several cartons of food. There were four or five crates of beer already on one of the lifeboats. Maggie was looking disapprovingly at this and Sarah felt a little uneasy and hoped there wouldn't be trouble.

Max appeared on deck to see them off and was insistent that Sarah should be in the lifeboat with Geoffrey. Then he ordered the bosun to get the boats away and they swung out on the davits and were soon in the water. As they began to pull away Sarah peered into the distance to try to spot the beach — anything to take her mind off Geoffrey.

7

Disturbing Developments

It would have been much more comfortable all round if Malcolm had come and Geoffrey had stayed on board doing anchor watch. Nancy would have been happy instead of sitting on her own at the back of the boat. Sarah was surprised she'd come at all. Maybe Malcolm, like Max, wanted time to himself and had persuaded her. Nancy would probably do anything to please Malcolm.

The boat Maggie was on rocked alarmingly as it made a turn and Sarah saw her lean on the cartons in front of her. They overbalanced and cans of beer rolled around in the bottom of the boat. Geoffrey was keeping a watchful eye as Sebastian helped Maggie to the other side of the boat and sat her down, whilst Kevin gathered up the cans and stowed them in the cartons again. Maggie looked shaken and not at all pleased at what had happened.

Then Geoffrey turned his boat and steered it steadily behind the other one, keeping close to it all the time. Sarah was glad now she was in his boat. Geoffrey inspired confidence and she could relax knowing he was in charge.

A long stretch of silver sand backed by palm trees appeared in the distance and Sarah felt a bubble of excitement. She'd never been to such an exotic place before. They anchored a distance from the beach and Geoffrey was soon out of the boat and up to his knees in water. He took her arm to help her out as it rocked alarmingly. 'Afraid you'll have to paddle ashore. Can't get the boat any closer.'

Their eyes met as he steadied her in the water, sandals in hand and skirt pulled up round her knees. He gave an amused smile and she looked away quickly then followed the others up the beach. It was quite a long walk and the stones hurt her feet in the flimsy sandals. Jess came trotting up beside her and Sarah was glad of the distraction.

'Can we climb over those rocks?' Jess asked.

Sarah glanced back at Maggie, who was sulking and giving Kevin a hard time. Taking Jess's hand and running up towards where Jess was pointing, she felt light-hearted and glad to be free of their petty squabbles.

Eventually they all settled on a silvery stretch of sand within a quiet cove with blue ocean lapping at the shore. Behind were spiky thorn bushes forming the scrub end of the jungle, with deserted tracks running into dense vegetation. Sarah found a shady spot beneath a palm tree and lent back against it to enjoy the view. A few of the men were kicking a ball round in a high-spirited attempt at football. Shelly was just about holding her own and called to Sarah to join in. Shelly was quick, agile and fearless as she tackled for the ball. Sarah was enjoying the opportunity to release her pent-up feelings, but approached the game more cautiously.

Nancy was sitting quietly on her own on the beach, watching; then Jess walked towards her, crouched beside her on the sand and showed her something she'd obviously found on the beach. Nancy looked at it with interest and they began to talk in an animated way and Nancy laughed. Sarah had never seen her laugh before.

She brought her attention back to the game and sprang up to catch the ball. Geoffrey effortlessly gripped it above her head then steadied her as she fell against him and she felt her heart begin to beat a little faster. Ben kicked it into the goal and there was an uproar of cheer from the winning side. Sarah flopped onto the sand and Geoffrey dropped down beside her, both panting and looking hot and flushed, not entirely due to the exertion on Sarah's part.

'We must be mad. It's true what they say about mad dogs and Englishmen,' she said, trying to sound light-hearted, when her whole being wanted him to hold her again.

Geoffrey laughed and leant back on his elbows. 'I enjoy these days. It's good to have a bit of normality. Things can get out of kilter when we're all cooped up on a ship.'

Joe came over to join them and overheard what was said. 'You can say that again. There's something very odd going on in the catering department for a start.'

Sarah glanced at Geoffrey. He was looking at Joe intently but said nothing. Then he shook his head, got up and walked away.

Joe sat beside Sarah and began to run sand through his fingers. 'I wish I could go home right now. I'm worried about Jenny. There's something she's not telling me.'

'How do you mean, Joe?'

His voice was edgy. 'She came with

me last year. We had a great trip. I was going to bring her again next trip. Only now we're having a baby, she won't be able to come for years.'

Sarah sighed and shook her head. 'That's always a problem, isn't it, with men at sea?'

Joe looked at her. 'Yes, but it's worth it to have a kid, isn't it?'

Sarah swallowed. 'Of course.'

'But Jenny didn't seem to feel that way. I've never known her that upset.' He went quiet and looked away, then turned to her, his voice tight with emotion. 'She didn't want to keep the baby.'

Sarah's heart gave a lurch.

Joe jumped up and started kicking the ball along the beach. Sarah watched in shock at what he'd said and hoped he was overreacting.

Shelly and Will were wandering up the beach and Ben was sitting on his own, morosely plucking at a piece of seaweed. Eventually Sarah got up and went and hunkered down in the sand beside him. 'What's up, Ben?'

He kept his head down and said nothing.

Joe came over to retrieve his ball and stood looking down at them. 'Coming for a dip, mate?'

Ben shook his head. Joe shrugged, looked questioningly at Sarah, then ambled off again. She watched him wander to the water's edge and splash his feet in the waves.

'Go and get some food, Ben,' Sarah said as she saw Kevin unpacking the picnic.

He ignored her so she gave up and joined the others. Shelly was chattering happily to Will, who was lazily crunching on a large apple. Nancy was sitting quietly eating a roll and not taking any notice of anyone. Sarah took a chicken leg from the coolbox and went to sit on the sand beside her but Nancy continued to stare out to sea and Sarah couldn't get her into conversation. Eventually she gave up and moved into the shade of a clump of trees. Sebastian was sitting alone some way from the others, trimming and then lighting a large cigar. Sarah looked away, not wanting to attract his attention. She didn't like the man and was determined to keep as far away from him as possible. Joe came back up the beach and poked around in what was left of the food, then shouted to Ben to come and have some. There was a lull in the conversation and everyone looked towards Ben. He immediately turned away from their staring faces.

When the conversation resumed, Shelly got up and slowly walked towards Ben, her face flushed and pretty but her eyes serious. She knelt down and said something to him. He looked at her accusingly. They spoke quietly — tense, short sentences interspersed with long silences. Shelly began to speak more intensely. Ben had his head bent, stubbornly determined to nurse his grievance. Eventually Shelly jumped up, sighed, shook her head and came back to the group, carefully placing herself beside

Joe and not Will.

'What's up with him?' Joe asked.

'He's stupid and pig-headed and obstinate,' Shelly said, her tone making it clear that further conversation on the subject was unwelcome.

Sarah knew now what the problem was. Of course, Ben and Shelly. He obviously had taken a shine to her and Shelly, being an outgoing girl, was friendly with everyone. Ben had read the wrong signals and seeing her with Will had made him jealous.

Sarah had tried to avoid Geoffrey during the afternoon but now her eyes were drawn to where he was playing with Jess at the water's edge. She wanted to join them but knew she mustn't. He caught her eye and smiled, said something to Jess, picked up the ball and walked up towards Sarah. She felt her pulse race and didn't know what to do. There was nothing she could do. So she smiled at him as he approached and he sat on the sand beside her.

'Enough of that for today,' he said.

She had to keep the conversation easy, not show any emotion. 'Children do wear you out. And Jess is certainly a lively one.'

'Well, you should know as you spend most of your time with them,' he laughed.

'Used to,' she corrected.

'But you're going back to it, aren't you?' He gave her a questioning look.

'I think I have to. I can't spend my life waiting for Max to come home. But he won't like it.'

'Is it what you want, though?'

She sighed. Did Max ever consider what she wanted? Geoffrey looked at her in a way that told her he knew exactly what she was thinking but said nothing.

She leant back on her elbows. It was quiet now except for the wash of the waves on the sand. Everyone was resting. Geoffrey stretched out and seemed to doze off, so she got up and walked along the beach.

The deserted tracks leading through the jungle looked cool and inviting. Black and yellow birds fluttered amongst the foliage and she could hear the whooping of gibbons in the kapok trees overhead. There were sounds she couldn't identify and, as a cool breeze rippled the fronds of the coconut palms, she stopped to breathe the fragrant air.

Ahead, the path seemed to lead into denser jungle and she was drawn into its secret depths. Struggling through the spiky undergrowth, she was aware of a rustling in the trees and stopped dead when she saw monkeys playing in the thick forest canopy above her. Then she heard a rustle and moved slowly in the direction of the sound and saw a large deer crunching on some leaves.

She was really here, the other side of the world, in a Malayan jungle. It seemed incredible that someone so ordinary as herself should be alone in such a place and she could only think of the joy of writing it all down in a letter to her sister. Her mum would never believe half of what she told her. She'd think she was making it up.

It was cool in here and she was alone with her thoughts when she was aware of someone behind her and turned to see Geoffrey picking his way through the undergrowth. When he caught up with her he took her arm and turned her to face him, a look of annoyance on his face. 'What do you think you're doing?' he snapped.

'Just taking a stroll. It's lovely in here.'

'Sarah, you shouldn't wander off like that. You scared the life out of me.'

'Oh, don't be silly. I'm a big girl. I won't get lost.'

'Sarah, it's dangerous in here. This land is swarming with scorpions and snakes and there are all sorts of wild animals. Even these monkeys can be dangerous. I wish you'd told me what you were doing. Let's get back.'

She shrugged. 'Okay, but I think you're making a fuss about nothing.'

'You won't think that if you come

face-to-face with a tiger.'

She laughed, which only made him more angry.

'Sarah, Max made me promise to look after you today. He wouldn't be very impressed if he knew I'd let you wander off alone, would he?'

The joy drained from her and she stiffened. 'Oh, so you're acting on orders, are you?'

He tightened his grip on her arm. 'Sarah, you're making this difficult for me.'

She pulled away. 'Then let's get back to the others and you can tell him you did your duty.'

He put his arms on her shoulders and turned her back towards him. 'Sarah, why are you talking like this?'

She bit back the tears. Why was she behaving like some love-struck teenager? 'I'm sorry,' she managed.

He gathered her into his arms and she didn't resist. 'This is as hard for me as it is for you,' he whispered.

He held her close for a long time

and she relaxed against him, wanting the moment to last. Time stood still; the world receded. There was just Geoffrey holding her, caring for her, protecting her.

Eventually they began to walk back to the beach. Her heart was tight in her chest, her head in turmoil. The others were packing up and Sarah noticed the sky was quickly turning a bruised black colour and the sun had been blotted out. There was an ominous silence in the air as the darkness took over. Geoffrey registered the urgency and quickly organised them to get back to the boat.

'Will's got the first boat away,' Joe told him. 'Maggie was beginning to panic so we rounded up as many as we could to go.'

Huge raindrops began to splatter them. Waves were now crashing onto the beach and soon they were wading into the now turbulent water towards the moored boat. Geoffrey grabbed Sarah's hand and pulled her with him.

She was glad when she was installed safely on board, even though the vessel was pitching violently.

Joe settled himself beside her and Geoffrey took the helm, handling the boat with confidence in the difficult conditions. Soon they were riding the waves at an alarming rate and Sarah had to grip the side to stay on her seat. But she felt no fear with Geoffrey in control, even though he was having difficulty keeping a steady course. She heard him tell Joe they'd lost radio contact with the ship and Joe went up and stood beside him. The sky was black now and thunder cracked the air. A great sheet of lightning flashed across the water. Waves were lashing the boat and with every crack of the waves water roared over them.

Shelly scrambled over to sit beside Sarah and they huddled together for security and comfort. Ben noticed Nancy sitting very stiff and upright on her own at the side of the boat, her face tense as the spray splashed over her. He eased his way towards her, took her arm and helped her to sit beside Shelly and she didn't object but huddled with the rest of them. Nobody spoke. It was all they could do to stay put and hold on. Still Sarah felt safe with Geoffrey handling the boat. Yet however hard she peered through the lashing rain she could see no sign of the *Melbourne*. Shelly was shaking as she clung onto her and Ben sat staring ahead of him, a picture of misery.

★　★　★

Max sat in his room reading, but he couldn't concentrate. He put the book down, went over to his cupboard and brought out the whisky bottle. He'd looked forward to this day with his room to himself again, but now all he could think about was what Sarah was doing and when she'd be back.

What would she be doing now? Romping on the beach like a child, no doubt. Probably with Geoffrey. The thought of his chief officer having fun with his wife upset him. Yet he could have been there with her. Remorse overwhelmed him.

Darkness fell on the room and he glanced out of the porthole to see heavy clouds moving rapidly across the sky. The wind was gathering strength and large raindrops began to splatter the glass. He quickly pulled the weather door closed and secured the portholes. It was going to be one of those tropical storms that could blow up instantly in this area and wreak havoc, then just as suddenly die down.

The ferocity of the wind was increasing by the second, causing the ship to roll and creak on its anchorage. But Max's concern was for the small boat which would now be bringing his wife back across the harbour.

He paced up and down the room and, as his agitation grew with the intensity of the weather, he pushed open the door again as a great flash of lightning lit up the deck and seconds later thunder split the sky in two. He forced his way against the onslaught of the wind and the stinging rain to look over the side of the ship for any sign of the lifeboat returning.

What he saw sent blood rushing to his head and he felt his whole body tense with shock and fear. The white, portholed side of a huge cruise liner loomed astern and was about to hit the *Melbourne* on its port beam.

He was up the ladder three steps at a time and onto the bridge. The wheel house was empty. Where was the second mate? Why hadn't he been alerted? Max was out on the wing instantly and glaring at the huge bulk that was about to buckle the side of his ship. He raced back inside the wheel house and grabbed the speaking tube to make contact with the engine room. The third engineer answered, then the chief was on the other end and alerted to the problem.

Mac nearly knocked Malcolm over as he barged into the chartroom. Max glared at him, his face thunderous, barely able to spit out his orders, then he battled his way out onto the wing of the bridge again to peer through the squall. Officers on the cruise liner were scurrying fore and aft, shouting excitedly to one another. Another flash of lightning showed a sailor legging it down the main deck after frantically ringing the foc'sle bell.

The bosun had the whole crew out now. Two sailors on the deck below were struggling towards the bridge ladder and Max bellowed at them. They turned and ran back to help the bosun work the windlasses to raise the anchor. Malcolm was at the wheel and Max rang for full ahead but he could see no chance of manoeuvring out of the collision. He stood helpless, waiting for the engines to begin to power the bow-thrusters to manoeuvre the ship to safely.

It was no good. The other vessel began to swing violently into them as the storm lashed her decks. It would strike near number four hatch above which the derricks were swinging with the motion of the ship. Any minute now they'd feel the impact — that horrific grating, crunching, nightmare he'd relived a million times.

His mind went back to that last time, all those years ago, and he felt the sweat pouring down his face and back. The cracking and splintering as the impact had made itself known; how the whole ship had shivered and trembled. All the legal formalities that followed. And this time he was master of the ship. He could not let it happen again.

The sea was in turmoil, surging over the well decks, grey and dreadful, slashing its fury on both ships. He peered into the squall with radar intensity but did not pick up any sign of the tiny lifeboat. Then he turned to observe the white liner and to his relief saw the great white side slowly but steadily making distance between them. They must have their engines full astern and were slowly moving away.

He stared in disbelief. They hadn't touched. His ship was safe.

This fleeting moment of relief gave way to an anxiety worse than any he had ever experienced. Where was his wife? He sought refuge once more in the shelter of the wheelhouse, water dripping down his collar and from his hair into his eyes, but he felt nothing but anger and fear. The radio officer was constantly trying to contact the small boat but without success. Max had never felt so helpless and afraid.

The bosun was making his way back along the foredeck, struggling with the wind and the roll of the ship. Max stood firmly beside Malcolm as he manoeuvred the ship out of danger, then he went back onto the wing of the bridge to ensure the two ships were safely apart.

* * *

Jess's fear was quickly forgotten as she helped her mother up to their cabin and sat her on the bunk.

'I knew we shouldn't have gone,' Maggie grumbled. 'I didn't think we'd see this ship again. They call it a lifeboat. I've never been so terrified in my life.'

Jess was rubbing her face and hair with a large white bath towel.

'Take that wet dress off, Jess. Pass me the other towel. I'm soaked to the skin.'

Kevin came into the room, his face full of concern. 'Are you all right, love?' He patted Maggie on the shoulder.

'You might well ask,' she said, edging away from his touch. 'A lot of interest you showed down there in that boat. Jess could have been swept overboard.'

'I had to help. It was all hands to for a while.'

'Huh! Always an excuse.' She got up and walked over to the wardrobe and pulled out a long towelling wrap.

Kevin watched helplessly. 'Why not have a nice hot shower? You'll feel better then.'

'I'm not cold,' Maggie snapped. 'I've got a splitting headache and I need to lie down. Perhaps you can look after your daughter for a while.'

'Well, I've just got to — '

Maggie stared at him coldly. 'Useless to ask you anything. Useless. That's what you are.'

Kevin left the room and bumped into Max in the alleyway.

'Where's the other boat?' Max demanded.

'Should be back any time. We left just ahead of them.'

'What do you mean?' Max roared. 'What's happened to the other boat? You must have seen it. Was my wife on that boat?'

'Yes, I believe so, sir. Maggie wanted to get back when the weather took a turn for the worse, so we set off ahead. Geoffrey rounded up the rest.'

Max was too anxious to argue. All he wanted was Sarah back on board. Nothing else mattered. He raced back onto the bridge. 'Lower the port lifeboat,' he ordered Malcolm.

Malcolm stared at him in disbelief. 'Sir?'

Max thumped his hand down on the ledge. 'That's an order.'

'Yes, sir. Who will man it, sir?'

'Assemble a crew. I'll take her out myself.'

Malcolm backed off at the rage confronting him.

Then Max took a deep breath and in a chillingly calm voice said, 'I am going to look for my wife. Do you understand? She is out there and in danger and I intend to find her and bring her safely back on board.' Then he lost it again and roared, 'Now do as I say. At once!'

Malcolm shot down the ladder, off the bridge. By the time he found the bosun he was shaking.

The bosun looked stunned. 'What? He wants to take the other lifeboat out? He's not thinking straight. What's the point? Those boats are unsinkable and they have radios and flares. He can't leave the ship in this weather. He's crazy.'

'It's an order,' Malcolm said. 'Sarah's

on board the second boat and it's not back. We've sent out a mayday but he's intent on going out himself.'

They heard a roar from the wing of the bridge and both jumped to attention. Malcolm leapt back up the ladder onto the bridge. Max was in a cold sweat. 'We've lost radio contact. Get the boat away.'

Malcolm nodded. Nancy was on that boat. He trusted Max, and whatever it took they had to get her back safely.

Max peered anxiously into the watery brightness, but saw no sign of the boat. He paced up and down the bridge while the crew readied the lifeboat, his long-sighted vision focused on the distant sea, alert to any speck that might give him hope. He'd stay out there all night if he had to, until he found Sarah.

Then he saw what he was looking for and his face creased into a smile.

8

Worrying Times

When Sarah came into the room dripping water, her hair hanging raggedly and her dress clinging to her legs, Max was listening to a symphony on the radio. He looked up, half smiling. 'Have you enjoyed your picnic?'

She stared at him for a moment, then fell into his arms and they clung together in laughter and relief.

* * *

Once she'd dried off Max poured a whisky and soda and they sat out on deck to watch the sun set in a clear blue sky with no trace of the trauma that had sent them into panic.

'It all happened so quickly,' Sarah said.

'That's the way in these parts. But you were in good hands.'

She gave him a quizzical look. 'Geoffrey wouldn't let me get into the first lifeboat. He told me you'd said I had to stay with him. Why was that?'

'Because I knew you'd be safe with him.'

'But you knew the others would be safe, too.'

'Of course. I wouldn't have allowed it otherwise. But you are my wife, Sarah. Logic doesn't come into it. I had to know Geoffrey was looking after you. And he did a good job.'

She got up and put her arms round him as he sat in the chair and he drew her to him. 'Max, I do love you.'

* * *

Later that evening Sarah went out on deck to savour the cool night air, to stare up at the stars and across the gentle motion of the sea. It instilled in her a peace she had rarely experienced and she never tired of this nightly routine before bed.

On her way back she found Malcolm sitting on one of the hatch covers, smoking a cigarette.

'I hear you had a pretty scary afternoon,' she said.

He groaned. 'You heard about it, then?'

'Lucky escape by the sound of things.'

'Yes,' he said, looking away from her.

'Max said you were on the bridge at the time. Must have been a bit alarming seeing a huge thing like that about to hit the ship.'

'Yes,' he said again. This wasn't like Malcolm. He was usually friendly and talkative. When he looked at her, his face in the moonlight was tense. 'Did he say anything else?'

She frowned. 'He has to write lots of reports, which doesn't please him.'

He took a long draw at his cigarette and looked straight ahead into the distance.

'You're bound to be shaken by it. Fortunately nothing happened. I shouldn't worry too much.'

He stood up. 'I'll worry when I haven't got a job.' Then he strode off.

Sarah told Max about their conversation when she went in. He looked up at her from his desk chair, where he was relaxing with a glass of whisky. 'He was negligent, Sarah. He knows that. Negligence can cost lives at sea. He needs to worry.'

She perched on the settee, feeling a little concerned. 'Could he lose his job?'

Max shook his head. 'No, it won't come to that. Do him good to stew a bit. He has the makings of a good officer but he's a lot to learn.'

'But they may not give him that chance.'

'And who are they?'

'You have to report to the company, don't you? They may not see it the way you do.'

'They probably wouldn't. Which is why I shall be sparing with the details. Nobody was hurt and no damage done. The situation was handled efficiently by all on board our ship. That is all they need to know.'

'You mean you won't mention his negligence in your report?' Sarah asked.

'I shall write my report as I think fit.'

Sarah shook her head and smiled.

Max frowned. 'I don't think I have to tell you that anything said between us in this room is strictly confidential.'

'Max, of course I know that. But I wish he didn't have to live with the worry for the rest of the voyage. He really thinks he's in big trouble.'

He got up and went to pour himself another drink. 'I'm sure you could find a way of letting him know without compromising my position. He's quite a bright fellow. I think he could take a hint.'

She felt her heart swell with love. Max was letting her deal with it in her own way, knowing she wouldn't let him down.

'The one I'm worried about now is young Geoffrey,' Max said, handing her a glass. 'Had word his child's ill. Radio officer got the message. He's in hospital with some infection.'

Sarah tensed. 'Is it serious, do you think?'

'I hope not. I don't want him moping around with his mind on other things. I need one officer I can rely on.'

★　★　★

Next morning Sarah saw Geoffrey pacing the deck and went down to him. When he saw her he walked towards the rail and stared out over the sea. She stood beside him. 'Max told me last night about Simon.'

He didn't move, didn't speak.

'Children are always going down with something.' She wanted so much to comfort him.

He turned and looked at her, his face grim, his mouth hardly able to form the words. 'It's serious, Sarah. This isn't some normal childish illness. He's in intensive care.'

There was so much anguish in his

face she hardly knew how to respond. 'What is it? Do they know?'

He shook his head. 'No. when I spoke to Louise on the ship-to-shore radio she said they were working on getting his temperature down. She sounded distraught. He's three years old, Sarah. I ought to be there with them, not on some ship at the other side of the world.'

'Will the company fly you home?'

'If it gets worse they may do. I'll insist if things haven't improved by tomorrow.' He walked away, down the ladder and disappeared behind one of the hatches. Pain cut through her as she watched him, knowing there was nothing she could do.

* * *

The atmosphere on board was tense as they berthed alongside the dock in Penang and waited for news of the child. Geoffrey went about his duties in silence. Malcolm was nowhere to be seen and Nancy kept her distance as well, appearing only at mealtimes and then quickly disappearing again.

Sarah wanted to reassure Malcolm that he wasn't in serious trouble but there hadn't been a chance. She worried about Nancy, too. It wasn't good for her to shut herself away like that.

The ship was quiet now that cargo work had finished for the day and all the various officials had gone home. Sarah walked slowly round the deck deep in thought, then she heard Jess giggling. She peered round the hatch and to her amazement saw Jess pushing Nancy on the swing, a contented smile on her face as her long skirt swished in the breeze. Sarah smiled to herself. At least she didn't have to worry about her.

Eventually word came that Geoffrey's son was responding to treatment and was out of danger. Sarah had wanted to talk to him all day but every time she caught a glimpse of him he'd been dashing around with a sheaf of papers in his hand, then he was on deck with the bosun overseeing the loading of cargo into the holds. Then he'd been in some dispute with a stevedore. He'd looked tired and stressed, not his normal relaxed self.

Finally she tracked him down now that work for the day had stopped. He was alone, checking the hatch covers, and seemed more at peace with himself but didn't smile as she approached.

'I hear you've had good news,' she said.

He stood and looked at her. 'I had a long phone call with Louise. He's doing well.'

'I'm so pleased,' she said.

He gave her a dejected look. 'She sounded so far away and lonely. I should be with her, Sarah. She's having to cope with it all alone.'

'Why don't you ask if you can be relieved and go home?' Sarah said.

He shook his head slowly. 'It has to be something a lot more serious than a sick child for that to happen.'

'There is nothing more serious than a sick child,' Sarah insisted.

'Sarah, you said yourself how children are always going down with something. He's on the mend. The company can't send their officers home every time a child has a temperature.'

She knew he was right. He continued to inspect the hatch covers and then wandered off further down the deck and she was left feeling rejected and hurt.

* * *

She woke with a heavy heart next morning and could have hugged Max when he said he would take her ashore. It was just what she needed to take her mind of all the tensions on board.

They took a taxi into town and Max hailed a trishaw.

'Where are we going?' Sarah asked.

'I'm taking you to Snake Temple. You seem to like unusual things, so communing with the vipers may amuse you.' He gave her a mischievous grin.

She shuddered at the thought but then decided he was joking and relaxed.

A wizened old man drew his trishaw up beside them and gave a gummy smile. 'Good day, Tuan.'

Max instructed him in Malay, a language he seemed at ease with. The trishaw wheels made a whirring sound that mingled with the wheezing of the grizzled old man as they sped along jungle roads, past rice fields with women bent over the crops and then on through small coastal communities where children played barefoot on boarded areas above the water level.

Sarah felt the old man shouldn't be doing such arduous work. He seemed so frail as his sandaled feet struggled to propel them along the rough road. She was glad when he finally eased his creaking trishaw to the base of the white stone steps of the temple. He gave a delighted grin when Max pressed a hefty tip in his hand and Sarah felt a little easier.

Stalls selling food, souvenirs and clothes, straw hats and colourful parasols littered the forecourt of the small pretty temple, its golden pagoda roof sparkling in the sunlight.

'The Temple of the Azure Cloud,' Max announced.

Sarah looked at him.

'Another name for it. After the colour of the Penang sky.'

She looked up and saw what he meant. The sky was a perfect clear blue.

The prayer hall was filled with the smoke of burning incense. 'Keeps the vipers calm so they don't bite,' Max said.

She realised he hadn't been joking when one of the red-robed Buddhist monks placed a green and yellow viper in her hands and exchanged a conspiratorial smile with Max.

'Don't worry, it's had its venom removed. He's handing you one of the tame ones,' Max assured her.

The monk laughed and coiled it round her shoulders. After a momentary shudder, she touched its soft warm skin and watched with fascination as it curled round her arms and looked up into her eyes, and her fear vanished.

There were small vipers all over the altar and out in the courtyard coiled in the branches of fruit trees. One of the monks was trying to explain and Max interpreted. 'He's saying they used to live in the jungle and came into the temple when the trees were felled. Now they're regarded as guardian spirits.'

Back on the ship she was happily content to sit and watch the sun set on a perfect day. One she had spent with Max.

★   ★   ★

Over the next few days in Penang the ship was busy discharging and loading cargo. Max was in constant demand, their room always full of people wanting something from him. First the shipping agent wanted information about the incident at the anchorage, reports, forms signed. Then officials from Customs and Immigration needed to see him and the chief steward produced store declarations for him to sign. Sarah felt in the way and escaped onto the only bit of deck that was relatively peaceful and busied herself reading and writing letters home.

She was glad when they set sail and the ship settled into its normal routine. Maggie managed to get her darts tournament underway and games were played throughout the short passage to Port Kelang. Sarah was beaten in the first round, not ever having played darts before. Maggie was right: it did bring the men together, and there was a lot of banter in the bar after the matches. Max got through to the finals but was beaten by Kevin, who was hailed champion.

Jess persuaded Sarah to play quoits on deck most days after her lesson and Sarah enjoyed the time they spent together. Jess had become a strong swimmer and was making a pretty good attempt at diving. Max spent several sessions with them explaining how various instruments on the ship worked. He was surprisingly patient and Jess enjoyed these times a lot.

Sarah was changing for dinner when Max came down from the bridge after docking in Port Kelang. 'The lads are going ashore for a drink tonight. They've asked if you'd like to go with them. Do you fancy that?'

'I'd love to, Max. It will be nice to have an evening out together.'

'I'll stay on board and hold the fort. Let the young ones enjoy a night out.'

Her face fell. He was doing it again. Fobbing her off with anyone who would take her ashore. Why didn't he want to come? He should want to. She sighed. He obviously preferred time on his own without her around.

The slight shift in his expression showed he'd registered her disappointment. 'I promise I'll take you ashore when we get to Singapore.'

* * *

The sky was darkening as Sarah joined Shelly at the top of the gangway. She'd put on a short orange and green print dress with a scooped neckline she'd bought from a stall in Penang because she loved the rich colours.

'Dusk comes so early now we're near the equator,' Shelly said. 'It took me a bit to get used to it.' She looked wonderful in a flared orange miniskirt and stretch bandeau top, her hair tumbling around her shoulders in a fiery mass.

Sebastian was standing a little way from them, talking to Will. Sarah shook her head in amusement at the medallion resting on his tanned chest, the collar of his shirt turned up. He really did fancy himself.

'Ben not coming?' Sarah asked.

Shelly frowned. 'No, he seems a bit down. I've tried talking to him. He was all right until we had that picnic in Penang. Now he thinks I'm interested in Will.'

Sarah looked at her. 'And are you?'

Shelly stiffened. 'No, I am not. Not in that way.'

Sarah quickly changed the subject. 'I see Maggie's on her own. Must have left Jess with Kevin.'

'Oh, Maggie! Everyone's talking about her. You should hear them in the bar when she's not around. Even Kevin has a go. I feel sorry for her in a way. I don't think she's very happy, do you?'

Sarah sighed. 'She certainly seems to have some hang-ups. I don't think she and Kevin get on all that well. But then, it's such a strange life on board a ship like this. They may be completely different at home.'

'Not from what I've heard. Kevin says she only puts up with him because she likes the lifestyle he provides.' Shelly coloured and looked embarrassed. 'Do you know about Bangkok?'

Sarah was puzzled. 'What is this about Bangkok? I've heard the rumours.'

Shelly seemed unsure whether to continue, then decided to go ahead. 'He's got a Malay girl there. Had her for years. Everyone seems to know about it. Except Maggie, of course. She's not been on a trip with him for years so he gets away with it. But this time he won't. Evidently he gets these letters in pink envelopes when the mail arrives on board in Singapore and he's always waiting to grab them and he stuffs them inside his shirt and rushes off.'

Sarah didn't know whether to laugh or be horrified. In the end they both burst out laughing.

When Geoffrey appeared he took one look at the pair of them and let out a shrill whistle. Shelly gave him a mock cross look. 'Don't you start!'

He jumped back. 'What have I done? I'm only showing my appreciation of two attractive young women.'

Sarah smiled happily. 'Well, this one enjoys a bit of flattery. So carry on.'

Shelly pretended to frown at her. 'Don't encourage him.'

He looked pretty good himself in well-cut linen trousers, toned muscles showing beneath the fine cotton of his shirt. Sarah determined that this evening she would keep him at arm's length. He was back to his normal cheerful self and she had to control her feelings. This whole business had to stop right here.

They all bundled into a couple of taxis on the quayside. Sarah was squashed in the back with Nancy and Malcolm. The heat was stifling and she felt her hands clammy and her skirt sticking to her legs. But there was something magical about this balmy night air.

The road led onto dirt tracks with mangrove swamps on either side, the roots of these strange tropical trees showing above ground as a dark tangled mass in the fading light. They seemed to be getting deeper into the jungle when a cluster of small dwellings appeared and Sarah could see a dimly lit shack with lanterns glowing in the dark night. Eastern music mingled with murmured voices filtered through a bead curtain and the only other sound in the warm, humid air was the rhythmic croaking of tree frogs and the drone of unseen insects. Beyond were unfathomable depths of tropical jungle.

'Don't look so scared,' Geoffrey said as they got out of the taxi.

'I can't help thinking about what's out there. Tigers and elephants and wild boars. You were the one who scared me when we were in Penang. But at least it was daylight then and I could have seen them.'

He laughed. 'The tigers aren't interested in you. They rarely come out of the jungle.'

She grunted at him. 'Very reassuring.'

'The most dangerous things you'll come across tonight are mosquitoes. And they will definitely want to eat you.'

She was aware of the constant drone of the things in her ear. 'So how do I protect myself from them?'

'Lots of gin and tonic. They don't like the quinine.'

'Sounds a good deterrent to me. I'll

go along with that.'

When Geoffrey appeared from the bead-curtained bar it was with two Tiger beers. He handed Sarah a bottle, then produced a straw from his shirt pocket and smiled. 'Magid said to give this to Missy. I'm afraid they don't run to glasses.'

The night was humid, with crickets chirping in the undergrowth. Lanterns hung over the entrance, giving a mystical light below the star-spangled sky, and Sarah felt light-hearted and happy. She was coping well with Geoffrey, casual and friendly, the way it should be.

He wandered off to talk to Kevin. Maggie had tagged onto Nancy, who stood quietly listening, her thoughts elsewhere. Malcolm was standing outside the bar on his own, smoking a cigarette. Sarah saw her chance and went up to him. 'Max was talking about that business in Penang earlier.' She couldn't afford to waste time in case Nancy joined them.

He looked at her. 'Oh, yes?'

'He was complaining about all the paperwork involved.'

'And?'

'He was saying there should be no repercussions once that was done. That it was merely a formality.'

He straightened up and looked more alert. 'No repercussions? No blame?'

'That's right. I don't understand all these things. I shouldn't be talking about it, should I?'

'No, you shouldn't. And I haven't heard a word you've said.'

She gave him a knowing smile and he returned it.

'Better go and join the others,' she said. 'Enjoy your evening.'

'Thanks, Sarah. I will now.'

★ ★ ★

The afternoon before they were due to dock in Singapore, Sarah found Ben out on deck sitting in a quiet place to the stern of the ship behind the hatches, deep in thought. 'You're looking a bit glum, Ben. Feeling homesick?'

He gave her a blank look. 'Something like that.'

'I felt like that a few days ago. It seems to hit everyone at some stage.'

'Yes.' His expression didn't change. He got up and looked out over the sea, then turned and gave her a dejected look. 'Sorry, Sarah, got to get going.'

He ambled off, leaving Sarah feeling she shouldn't have disturbed him. It was hard to find somewhere on a ship like this where you could be miserable in private.

She went up onto the bridge to see if Max was there. He was talking to Malcolm, so she wandered into the chartroom and began to study the maps laid out there. Surrounded by sea most of the time, it was difficult to keep track of where they were. She pushed a dark strand of hair from her forehead. It was too hot. She'd never felt so hot.

Max came to see what she was doing, then went down from the bridge.

'I'll be out of your way in a minute,' she told Malcolm when he came in to look at the chart. 'I wanted to make a note of the ports for my diary and letters home. My sister likes a full account of everywhere I've been.'

Malcolm smiled. 'No worry. Take as long as you like.'

Shelly came up the ladder and joined him in the wheelhouse. They exchanged a few words, then she came into the chartroom and looked over Sarah's shoulder. 'Singapore next.'

Sarah straightened and smiled. 'I'm pleased someone else is as enthusiastic as I am.'

'It's only my second trip so I'm bound to be.'

'I've just seen Ben. He didn't seem very happy. Do you know what's worrying him?'

Shelly shook her head. 'He's just moody, that's all. Take no notice of him.'

That didn't sound like Shelly and Sarah wondered what was going on between them. She lowered her voice.

'How are things with Nancy?'

Shelly shrugged. 'Same really. She ignores me and talks to Malcolm. I just wish she wouldn't get in the way.'

Sarah frowned. 'How do you mean?'

'She makes me feel as if I'm the one who shouldn't be here.'

Shelly bounced back into the wheelhouse and Sarah got back to her chart and notebook. A couple of minutes later Nancy appeared on the bridge. Malcolm was pointing something out in the distance to Shelly. Nancy stopped and her whole body tensed. Then she walked over to them and they both turned quickly to face her. Shelly moved away from Malcolm and Nancy stood as close to him as she could. They began to talk together quietly. When Nancy went to fill the kettle, Malcolm spoke to Shelly and she looked up at him as if she was going to object, then shrugged and walked brusquely into the chartroom.

As she spoke her face crumpled and her voice quavered so that Sarah could barely make out what she was saying. 'He was explaining how the tug boats take us into port in the morning. Now he's told me to go down. Get some studying done.' She swallowed. 'I need the experience. That's what I'm here for.' She quickly walked away, but not before Sarah saw the tears coming.

Sarah drank the tea Nancy brought her, returned her cup to the table and told Malcolm she was going down. She could see that Shelly had been right. Nancy was upsetting things.

She started off walking round the deck, deep in thought. It was no good telling Max. Maybe she should have a word with Nancy, but that wasn't something she relished and she didn't want to be accused of interfering.

She stopped when she saw Max on the foc'sle deck with Jess. He was pointing to the windlass and demonstrating how the anchor could be winched up using the big, heavy wheel. Jess was staring at the hole in the red metal deck where the huge chain slid down. Then he had her leaning over the side, obviously looking at where one of the anchors hung in the bow of the ship. Jess was concentrating hard and asking questions. They didn't know she was there and she didn't want to disturb them so she turned and quietly walked away with a spring in her step.

9

Dilemma for Sarah

When they docked in Singapore everyone wanted to see Max. Customs officers, suppliers, shipping agents; there was always someone knocking on the door, wanting papers signed, questions answered. Out on deck the hatch covers had been removed and cranes were hoisting cargo into holds. Forklift trucks trundled along the quayside and men shouted above the noise of the machinery. Everyone was busy. Everywhere was noisy.

Sarah escaped from the room when a stevedore came in wanting to discuss some damaged cargo. She'd had enough of it for one day. As she passed the radio officer's room, he shouted to her through a mass of bodies and handed her a bundle of mail. 'Some for you there, Sarah. Leave the rest and I'll sort it later.'

'I'll deliver it if you like, Dave,' she offered, glad of something useful to do.

There was one from her sister, the distinctive blue air letter. Most of the bundle consisted of these flimsy blue squares. Except the small pink envelope that stood out amongst the rest, and Sarah smiled to herself and wondered if Maggie really did not know.

Everyone looked forward to the mail. Her mum and sister never missed a port. First stop was the galley and by the time she'd handed out letters to the cook, galley boy and three of the stewards, Joe had opened his and was reading it. He looked up as she passed, his face tense, then crumpled the letter and shoved it in his pocket. Sarah felt it wasn't appropriate to question him with so many in the room, so quickly looked away and continued along the alleyway.

She was delighted to see three letters for Ben and hurried along to his room. 'Some folk are popular. Is it your birthday?'

'Actually, yes,' he said sheepishly.

Sarah handed him his mail. 'You'll have to buy everyone a drink, you know.'

Ben looked alarmed. 'Will I?'

'Of course you will. Don't be so mean,' she teased.

Ben was quick to defend himself. 'I didn't mean that. I mean . . . well . . . does everyone have to know it's my birthday? You know what they're like.'

She gave him a warm smile. 'Don't worry, I'll fix it. Nothing terrible will happen. You've had your ducking in the pool. You're an old-timer now, you know.'

He managed a smile but didn't look convinced.

Kevin nearly jumped on her when she turned into his alleyway. He grabbed the letters, sorted through them, pulled out the one he'd been looking for and stuffed it down his shirt. Then he gave her a sharp, angry look. 'What's wrong with Dave? He usually delivers.' He was off down the alleyway without waiting for an answer.

She was surprised there were no letters for Geoffrey but supposed he'd taken his already. The last letters delivered, she hurried back to the room to change. The mini bus going into town would arrive soon and she wasn't going to miss an opportunity for some shopping.

Max looked up from his desk as she came through from the bedroom and thought how lovely she looked in the floral dress with her dark, shiny hair bobbing round her heart-shaped face. The pale lemon suited her now she had some colour from the sun.

Joe came in with a tea tray and put it down on the table. He didn't speak or look up. Something in that letter had obviously upset him.

Sarah poured the tea and handed a cup to Max. 'It's Ben's birthday today. Can we go down to the bar after dinner this evening and have a drink with him? I've asked a few of the others and they all said they'd be there and cook's going to make a cake.' She held her breath for his answer and was pleasantly surprised when he agreed.

'Make sure you're back on board in good time, then.'

'I can only come when the bus brings us.'

'Of course, sweetheart. You have a good day. Buy something nice for yourself.'

*　★　*

Once in town the men went their separate ways. Maggie had left Jess behind on the ship again with Kevin. As she seemed to know the best places to shop, Sarah and Nancy followed her. Everywhere was a riot of sounds, smells and colour. Tiny Chinese women in patterned trousers and bright tunics stood beside street stalls topped by colourful parasols; Tamil traders in turbans, white shirts and baggy trousers sold rattan bowls of spices and sweetmeats; and there were hundreds of ramshackle cabins made of plywood and corrugated iron offering a bewildering array of clothes, toys, and incense.

Sarah was pleased Nancy had come with them even though she said little and kept her distance. They followed Maggie up some steps along a monsoon drain onto a raised street where small shops spilled their wares onto the pavement. The shop Maggie wanted was packed tight with electrical goods and racks of glittering watches displayed beneath glass counters.

The proprietor was a tubby bespectacled little man. 'Good watches. Best in Malaysia. Shockproof, dustproof.' He rattled on, but Maggie took no notice of him.

'I want a radio,' she told him after examining the contents of the shop thoroughly.

He quickly unlocked a cabinet and took several down to show her, all the time extolling the virtues of the different ones. She picked one out, then began to haggle with him. Nancy looked embarrassed but Sarah was fascinated. Eventually Maggie was satisfied she had a bargain and handed over the cash.

Nancy was looking at the watches but backed away when the tubby little man approached her.

'Do you want a watch?' Sarah asked her.

Nancy looked into the glass case and frowned. 'I'm not sure.'

Sarah gave her an encouraging smile. Maggie waited impatiently by the door. The proprietor hovered. Nancy looked uncomfortable. Then she turned towards the door. 'I think I'll leave it.'

Sarah touched her arm. 'If you want one, this seems a good shop.'

Nancy looked undecided. 'I don't like bartering. It's so demeaning and I don't think I could do it.'

'I'd be no good at it, either. But we have an expert with us.' Sarah looked towards Maggie.

She came back into the shop. 'Right, girl, which one do you want?'

Nancy frowned. 'It's for Malcolm. That's why I came.'

'Which one do you think he'd like?' Sarah encouraged.

Nancy wavered. Sarah pointed to one in the glass cabinet. 'I think he'd like that one.'

Nancy looked at it, then at Sarah. 'Yes, I'll have that one.'

Maggie swung into action and soon arrived at a price she considered fair. Nancy paid and Maggie strode towards the door. She'd obviously had enough of dithering. Nancy gave Sarah a restrained smile as they followed her.

* * *

For Ben's party Sarah changed into a long dress in emerald green. The material draped gracefully and showed off her shapely figure. She asked Max if he thought it was suitable. He raised an eyebrow and told her she looked stunning. She added some dangly earrings and a necklace. She wanted Ben to feel his birthday was special and worth dressing up for.

By nine o'clock the bar was full and noisy.

'Do you like it? I bought it in Change Alley. Only twenty-six dollars. Funny little fellow wanted fifty,' Maggie's voice piped out.

'And the dress — is that new?' George asked.

'Yes, I managed to get him down to twenty. It's good quality cotton.'

'Very becoming, Maggie. Of course you can carry off these bright colours so well,' George said.

Kevin was looking with distaste at the garish colours in the dress as he poured a pint. 'Expensive junk, that's all it is.'

Malcolm came in with Nancy. She wore a simple cotton dress with no jewellery and stood silently waiting for her drink, serene and self-contained as always. When she saw Sarah she smiled and Sarah noticed Malcolm was wearing the watch.

'Come on, Kevin. Cheer up. At least the beer's on Ben,' Malcolm joked.

Kevin looked round. 'Where is the

lad, anyway? He's not on watch, is he?'

They scanned the room.

'Hey, Will, where's Ben?' Kevin asked.

Will shrugged and glanced round the room. 'No idea. You know Ben. Strange lad. Can't make him out at all.'

Shelly bounced into the bar and there was silence. She wore a short red frilly skirt and matching off-the-shoulder top. Every eye was on her and Shelly stopped in her tracks, her face turning the colour of her outfit.

'Wow!' Kevin said. 'Been shopping?'

'I'm not on watch for three hours. I don't live in that uniform, you know,' she said defensively.

Will jumped up to give her his seat. 'What will you have to drink?'

'Shandy, please,' she said, smiling up at him.

Nancy eyed the outfit and moved a little closer to Malcolm. She took the glass of wine handed to her and sipped it slowly.

'Where's the lad, then?' Kevin asked Shelly.

She looked round and shrugged.

Kevin nudged Sebastian. 'Come on, let's find him.'

Shelly noticed Kevin's expression and jumped up. 'I'll get him.'

Will had her drink in his hand. He watched her go, then sat down by Maggie. The conversation buzzed and Kevin was kept busy behind the bar. It was half an hour before Shelly appeared again with Ben.

'Come on there, lad,' Kevin said, beckoning him over to the bar. 'Pour the lad a beer.'

Everyone raised a glass and made the usual comments, some not so polite. Shelly stood beside Ben, radiantly pretty and smiling. Cook came in bearing high a magnificent cake complete with burning candles. They all cheered as Ben was forced to blow them out. He looked happy, though, and Sarah felt those two young people had resolved their differences.

As the excitement died down and normal chatter resumed, Shelly and Ben talked together quietly, his head bent to hear her, more relaxed than Sarah had seen him. Amazing what a pretty girl could do for a man, she thought.

As the evening drew on Max made his excuses and left, telling Sarah to stay if she wanted. He said he had things to do but she guessed he just wanted time to himself to read his book. Others were leaving but she was reluctant to go back to the quietness of the room with Max sitting under his desk light, not wanting to be distracted with conversation. She lingered and talked to anyone who was still there and sober. She'd been watching Geoffrey for some time. He was sitting on his own in a corner drinking pint after pint. Eventually she got up and went to him.

Slow, romantic music played quietly in the background and she swayed in time to its rhythm as she put her glass down on the table beside his. He stared vacantly at her and tried to get up, staggering a little, and eventually made it round the table. She watched his awkward movements and then suddenly found herself in his arms. His cheek was close to hers as he swayed and stopped, then moved on again into the middle of the room. She held on to him, trying to steady him and talk to him, but he wasn't listening.

Johnny Nash was singing 'Tears on my Pillow' and Sarah tensed. Geoffrey was holding her close and she knew if she pulled away he'd probably fall over. So she relaxed into the rhythm of the music and tried to ignore her troubled conscience.

Suddenly he took her arms firmly and released himself, looked at her with glazed eyes then, leaving her standing there, he walked unsteadily to the door and left the room. She went after him, fearing he was going to do something silly. When she got out on deck he was standing staring into space and swaying slightly. He looked at her with glazed eyes. 'Sarah, just leave me alone. Please.'

She stood silently watching him and wondering what she should do. He walked over to the rail and leant on it, staring at the lights on the quay. She went and stood beside him. 'Geoffrey, what's wrong?'

'Everything, that's what. My son's sick. My wife wants me to give up everything I've worked for. And I've fallen in love with someone I can't have. Is that enough?'

She couldn't answer and looked down into the inky depths of the water, feeling his pain.

Eventually he straightened up and she turned to face him. He seemed more sober, as if the fresh night air had revived him. 'Sarah, I'm sorry. I really shouldn't be talking to you like this.'

There was just enough light for her to search his eyes and there was so much pain there it made her own heart ache. 'Geoffrey, you know how I feel about you. We didn't ask for this to happen. But we do have to deal with it. It will all seem different once we're off the ship and life begins to get back to normal.'

'Sarah, what's normal? I can't see how any of this is going to feel different when we get back to Liverpool. I love you now and I shall love you then. And I think you feel it, too.'

'No, Geoffrey.' This was taking all her strength but it had to be said. 'I love Max. I always have and I always will. I do have feelings for you but they're different. We have to be strong for each other.'

The look he gave tore at her heart. Then he turned and made his way back inside, leaving her standing watching after him, her mind in turmoil.

When Sarah woke it was mid-morning and the dockside was buzzing with activity. Max had promised to take her ashore and she wanted, now more than ever, to spend time with him, away from the ship, away from Geoffrey.

Out on deck men were working cargo and the noise was deafening. She ambled into the room where Max was sitting at his desk, poring over papers. He turned when he heard her. 'Not like you to sleep all day.'

She went over to him and put her arms round his neck from behind as he returned to his work. 'I'll be ready when you are,' she said, nuzzling his cheek.

He swivelled round in his chair to face her. 'Ah, now, I'm not sure I'll make it after all.'

'Max!' Disappointment overwhelmed her.

He sighed. 'Could do without this lot.'

'What's happened now?' She looked at the form he was filling in, saw the name and tensed. 'What's this about Joe?'

'Nasty accident, I'm afraid. Fell down some steps and seems to have injured himself rather badly.'

Her body tensed. 'Where is he?'

'He's off to hospital. The medics didn't like the look of him so they strapped him onto a board and took him off. And now I've got yet more reports to write. It's a good job we were alongside.'

She gasped. 'Was he conscious?'

Max frowned. 'Yes, he did come round before they carted him off. Looks like we'll be a steward short for the rest of the trip. Don't expect they'll get him patched up in time for sailing.'

'What will happen to him? How will he get home?'

'They'll fly him back once he's recovered. That's if he does.'

An ice-cold shiver ran through her. 'Can I go and see him?'

Max stared at her. 'What for? He's in good hands.'

Sarah gripped the side of the door. 'He'll be terrified. Imagine how you'd feel in a foreign country in a strange hospital with nobody you knew.'

'Part of the life, my love. We choose it and we have to live it.'

'But Max, it's the least I can do. How long are we here for?'

'A couple more days at most. Loading's going well. You can go tomorrow if you like. I'll arrange a car for you.'

'No, Max, I want to go today.'

He gave her one of his long, hard looks then shook his head slowly and smiled. 'You're a funny girl, Sarah. All right, I'll see what I can do.'

Sarah waited impatiently in the room while Max was gone. The minutes dragged on and her anxiety increased. If only Max would hurry up.

It was over an hour before he strode into the room. 'The agent will take you on his way back to town.'

'When?' Sarah asked.

'About an hour, I should think.'

'Couldn't I get a taxi?'

'No need for that. He'll drop you off at the hospital.'

But I want to go now, she nearly said, but held back, knowing how easily she could antagonise him. The hour dragged on to two.

She went out on deck and walked round to see if there was any sign of the agent. Maggie was standing at the top of the gangway with Jess.

'Where's that useless husband of mine? The taxi's picking us up in ten minutes.'

The last thing Sarah wanted was to share a car with Maggie and Kevin. Or even worse, to be held up whilst waiting for him. 'I think he's with Max. I'm not sure he's going to get ashore. This business with Joe has upset everyone.'

Maggie stared at her. 'Well, that's just not on!'

Sarah shrugged. 'Max can't get away either. It means one short on board. And there'll be reports to write.'

'I hope he's not expecting my Kevin to take over Joe's work.' She huffed and turned back to scan the dockside. 'What is it with your husband? Always checking up on everyone. You'd think he didn't trust them.'

Sarah couldn't see what this had to do with Joe, so exchanged a sympathetic look with Jess and moved on. But the question remained in her mind. Why was Maggie so concerned about Max checking up on Kevin and not trusting people?

Eventually she was being driven through the outskirts of Singapore towards the hospital. She had been looking forward to seeing the city. It was what she most enjoyed about going ashore: new places in different countries. But all she wanted now was to get to the hospital.

The car drew up outside and Sarah was taken to a small ward by a slim, pretty nurse. Behind a screen she saw Joe lying in bed, his eyes closed and looking grey and drawn. She touched his hand gently and he opened his eyes.

They didn't talk much, as every word seemed an effort for him. She touched his hand and it felt cold. He drifted in and out of consciousness and his voice was so quiet and halting she could barely make out what he was saying.

'I'm afraid, Sarah.'

She squeezed his hand.

'Will you stay with me?'

'I can't, Joe, but I'll come back tomorrow.'

He closed his eyes and she sat quietly beside him until a nurse came and asked her to leave. As she released his hand he opened his eyes and, grasping her arm, gave her an anxious look. 'There's a letter on my desk. Will you get it for me? I don't want anyone to read it. It's important, Sarah. Will you do it?'

It took all his strength and there was such urgency in his voice that she promised and left. As she sat in the taxi on her way back to the ship she didn't see the bustling streets. She didn't hear the noise of the traffic. She held her head as if to still the turmoil. How was she to do what he'd asked and not let anyone know? She'd promised. He'd be relying on her. It seemed so important to him. Max wouldn't understand. He wouldn't let her do it. She knew he wouldn't. Geoffrey would know what to do. But she couldn't go behind Max's back and tell Geoffrey.

Maybe she wouldn't have to do it. Joe could be back on board before they sailed. But what if he wasn't? The letter he wanted must be the one he was so angry about. She wondered what it contained to upset him so much and why he was so anxious nobody should read it. How was she to get into his room without anyone seeing her? And what would Max say when she told him she wanted to go back to the hospital tomorrow?

* * *

There was an atmosphere of gloom all over the ship that evening. Everyone was talking about Joe. But all Sarah could think about was how she was to get the letter.

She walked past Joe's room and tried the door, but it was locked. The only way she could think of was to wait until Max had gone to bed, then sneak down with his pass key. It seemed wrong but she'd promised Joe.

Max didn't feel inclined to go to bed early that night. He wanted to play chess with her and the game went on until midnight. When they did eventually go to bed she lay beside him until she was certain he was asleep, then crept out and pulled on a pair of shorts and a T-shirt. She quietly opened the drawer where she'd seen his bunch of keys and slipped out of the door, wishing she had never agreed to do it, but she had and now she must keep her promise.

As she crept along the lighted alleyways she was acutely aware of the ridiculous position she was putting herself in. Ships never slept. There was always someone on watch, always someone around, and what would they think of her tripping around half-dressed in the middle of the night? How could she ever explain herself to Max should he wake while she was gone? What if someone came along as she was opening Joe's door?

She closed her mind to all reason and continued making her way through the ship. Joe's room was three decks down and there were many alleyways to traverse before she reached it. Kevin's door was slightly open and the light on. She paused, not wanting to be seen, as voices floated out through the gap, and she could hear movement near the door. Maggie wasn't happy about something but their voices were low.

She heard Kevin say, 'Maggie, I am not taking that money. It's Joe's.'

Maggie's voice was hard. 'He wouldn't have it only for you. I don't know why you gave it to him in the first place. You said he didn't want it.'

'I did it to keep him quiet. He kept asking questions and I knew he was getting suspicious. And I think Max is on to us as well.'

'Right mess. How is it you never get anything right?'

'Leave it, Maggie, will you?' His voice was hard and Maggie didn't reply.

Sarah froze. She was afraid to move in case they heard her. Then the door closed and she could hear nothing more. Breathing again, she continued down the alleyway, reached Joe's room undetected, opened the door and closed it quietly behind her. His light was on but she could see no sign of the letter, just a crumpled envelope in his wastepaper basket.

She opened one of the desk drawers to see if he'd put the letter in there. After opening every drawer, there was still no sign of it. Some papers were sticking out from a row of books. Maybe it was there. She pulled them out to look and noticed a brown envelope wedged behind the books with just its end visible. Perhaps he'd hidden it in there and forgotten. She pulled it out and let out a gasp. It was full of bank notes. What was Joe doing with all this money?

Then, as she stared at it, she knew it was what Kevin had been talking about and her legs went weak. She stood with it in a shaking hand. She couldn't think what to do. She wanted to run back to her room and tell Max. But that wasn't an option. She stuffed it back behind the books and tried to calm herself, think straight, but she couldn't.

The crumpled letter was with the papers so she tucked that in her pocket. If Max was awake when she got back and wanted to know where she'd been she'd tell him everything. Joe shouldn't have asked her to do this.

She froze when she heard footsteps and her mind tried to invent a reason for being there. But she was lucky. The figure strode across the end of the alleyway, not looking in her direction, and she heard a door bang. It was Sebastian and, by his demeanour, he didn't seem too happy. But she had other things on her mind.

Max was still asleep when she reached their room so she put the letter in her handbag and crept into bed beside him. She needed to think. And in the darkness she lay awake until morning and still could not decide what to do.

10

Feelings Run High

Next morning Max seemed in high good humour. 'I want to take you to visit some very old friends of mine today. They live in Kuala Lumpur and they'll pick us up about ten. Wear something cool and cover up as we'll spend most of the day in an open boat. They want to take us to a prawn farm.'

Sarah was surprised and delighted. It all sounded very exciting. And it was something Max wanted to do. She thought about the letter she had to get to Joe and instantly dismissed it. Joe shouldn't have put her in this impossible position. She'd keep the letter and give it to him if he came back on board. Otherwise, she would just forget about the whole thing and pretend none of it had happened. She was going to enjoy a day with her husband and nothing was going to interfere with that.

Dressed in a long cotton dress and wide-brimmed straw hat, she was ready when Max appeared to tell her Jim and Marion were waiting for them on the dockside in their car. Max looked good as always in shorts and a polo shirt.

'Don't usually come this far afield,' Max said as they drove along the coast road to Kuala Lumpur. Jim and Marion were ex-patriots who had spent many years in Malaysia and were soon due to go back to the UK.

'Can't wait,' Marion said, hunching her shoulders and looking excitedly at Sarah, who was sitting beside her in the back seat. 'It can get very monotonous out here. I want a lovely little cottage in an English village.' She sighed deeply and Jim laughed.

They drew up beside a moored boat and Sarah was introduced to Faiz whilst his men loaded wooden crates of ice into the boat, and soon they were motoring along the river until they came to a huge lake surrounded by tropical jungle. They tied up beside a ramshackle wooden structure on its bank and Max helped Sarah up onto the veranda. Inside she could see two young Chinese women chopping vegetables beside a sizzling wok. They looked up and smiled and said something Sarah didn't understand so she smiled back.

'Faiz owns all this,' Jim explained as they sat on rattan chairs sipping ice-cold beer. 'Made his money supplying hotels with prawns.'

Sarah watched the boat motor out onto the lake while the men chatted and Marion went to help with the preparation of the meal. It was cooler on the veranda with a slight breeze drifting from the lake and shimmering the papaya trees overhead. Surrounded by the beauty of the tropical jungle, Sarah felt relaxed and happy. Max kept looking at her and smiling, away from his ship, more attentive, more like the old Max.

When Sarah asked Marion where the

toilet was she burst out laughing. 'You won't need your handbag, dear.' She pointed to a very tall tree with what looked like a tree house at the top. Sarah thought she was joking until Marion guided her through the jungle path to the base of a rope ladder. Then Sarah laughed, too. This really was going native.

The prawns, freshly caught and fried with the vegetables and herbs in the wok, were delicious. After eating they sat chatting and laughing over a plate of freshly sliced papaya. Sarah was sorry when they began to load the boat with the ice boxes, now full of prawns. The sun was setting as Jim drove them back to the ship. It had been such a lovely day with these lovely friends. And with Max.

* * *

The ship was to set sail next morning and Sarah still felt guilty about not having seen Joe again. She couldn't get his haunted look from her mind and wanted him to know she'd done what he'd asked and that nobody had seen his letter. She had no idea what it was he was so keen to hide. She suspected it was to do with Kevin and the money. And all this tied up with Maggie's comment about Max checking up on them. There was something going on and she didn't want to know. All she wanted was to get the letter to Joe and then forget about it. But she couldn't think how she could do this without rousing Max's suspicions.

She went out on deck to ponder the situation and was amazed and relieved to see Joe being escorted up the gangway. He was unsteady but at least he was back on board, which must mean there was nothing seriously wrong. Her heart lightened. She would be able to give him his letter and be free of guilt. And Max need never know anything about it.

★ ★ ★

Joe was sitting in a chair and looking much better when Sarah poked her nose round his door. He saw her and turned.

'How are you?' she asked.

Joe shrugged. 'My head aches and I feel dizzy when I stand up, but they said I'd be okay in a couple of days. Did you get the letter?'

She handed him the crumpled sheet.

'That's the one. Have you read it?'

'No, Joe, of course not.'

'Read it. I want you to.'

Her face creased into a frown as she read. He was waiting for her reaction.

'I can see why it's upset you. But Jenny's all right now. She didn't lose the baby. I'm sure she'll be fine. It happens all the time.'

'But she didn't seem too bothered, did she?'

'She wouldn't want to worry you.'

'I think she wanted to lose it. I think she might try again.'

'No, Joe!'

He became agitated. 'I told you, didn't

I? She didn't want the baby in the first place. But I do. I have to get home. Whatever it takes, I have to get home.'

Sarah had an uncomfortable feeling that Joe's fall might not have been an accident.

'And the money thing. I wanted to ask you about it.' He leant forward, his body tense, his hands shaking. 'It's really why I wanted you to get the letter. I didn't want anyone wondering about it and asking questions.'

'Does it have something to do with Kevin?' she asked.

He looked alarmed. 'How do you know?'

'I heard Kevin and Maggie talking.'

He put his head in his hands. 'They can have it back. I never wanted it in the first place. Kevin made me have it.' He stopped and his voice dropped. 'I shouldn't have taken it. I knew it was wrong. But I thought it would please Jen.'

Sarah looked back at the letter. 'Jenny's not happy about it, is she? She says so here.'

'Jen's really honest. And now I don't know how to get out of it. If Max finds out and I lose my job she'll never forgive me.'

'Joe, this is serious. Are you telling me Kevin's in some racket getting money from people who supply the ship with food?'

His voice came out as a mumble. 'He's up to his neck in it. Made me take it to keep me quiet. Said it would be okay.' He looked at her, his face a picture of misery. 'What am I to do, Sarah?'

She shook her head. 'I don't know, Joe.'

It was a relief when Shelly came in with an armful of magazines. 'Max said you're to take it easy for a day of two,' she told Joe.

Sarah forced a smile. Joe looked exhausted and closed his eyes, so they left him.

* * *

After dinner Sarah went out on deck in the cool of the evening air to sort out the turmoil in her mind. It was peaceful with just the sound of the sea and stars above in a vast dark sky. She could think more clearly. But the loneliness of the night weighed down on her and she wanted to talk to Geoffrey. She had to know what he thought she should do. There was nobody else she could ask.

Trying to numb her guilty mind, she walked zombie-like down the ladder to the deck below and into the accommodation where Geoffrey's room was. His door was closed so she knocked quietly and he called for her to come in. He was sitting on the edge of his settee, hands clasped between his knees, staring at the floor and, when he looked up, managed only a weary smile.

'What did you think of Joe?' she asked.

'Not good. I hope they know what they're doing, sending him back in that state.'

'Did he say anything to you?'

'He told me he had a headache. No

wonder. Poor sod had concussion.' He didn't seem disposed to discuss the matter with her further and looked back at his clenched hands.

She wanted to tell him everything that had happened and ask him what she should do. But he seemed so despondent she didn't feel she could burden him with more trouble. 'You seem a bit down.'

Geoffrey nodded, then looked up at her. 'Sarah, I'm sorry about the other night. I'd had too much to drink and I behaved badly.'

'I wish I could have been more help.' She perched on the settee beside him and he took her hand.

'You were a help just by being there and listening to me.'

'Have you heard from Louise?' she asked.

'Yes, it was short and to the point. Simon's on the mend. And that was about it.'

'I expect she's busy with two young children to look after.'

'There's more to it than that.'

She waited for him to continue.

'Sarah, I don't think my marriage is going to survive.'

'Geoffrey, don't say that. You're going through a rough patch. Once you get home it will all look different.'

'No, it won't. It wasn't good last time. She wants me to give up the sea and get a shore job. She hates me being away. She can't come with me and she feels trapped with the children.'

'Will you do that?'

'Sarah, the sea's my life. I can't imagine doing anything else. I've worked for years to get where I am. I'm due to get my command any time now. It's what I've always wanted, to be master of my own ship. I can't give that up.'

'Max is the same. He could never do anything else.'

'But you wouldn't ask him to, would you?' His face was distorted with pain.

'No, I wouldn't. It would destroy him.'

'He's a lucky man.'

'What will you do?'

He stood up and stretched to his full height and looked down at her. 'I don't know.'

They were silent for a moment.

'Sarah, thank you for listening. I promise I won't embarrass you again. I hope we can still be friends.'

She stood up and took his hands in hers. 'Of course we can. I don't know what I'd do if I couldn't talk to you. A ship can be a very lonely place.'

'Friends,' he said and kissed her hands.

She left Geoffrey, feeling there was nothing she could do or say that would make anything better. And she still didn't know what to do about Joe. She had to tell somebody. She ought to tell Max.

* * *

Geoffrey caught up with her as she paced round the deck on her morning walk next day. She stopped and stared at him. Instead of his uniform, he now had on a navy boiler suit over his white shirt, and a safety helmet instead of his uniform cap. But he did seem restored to his normal good humour.

She burst out laughing and he smiled. 'On my way to sound out number one deep tank.'

'Don't let me detain you, then.'

'What was it you wanted to know last night about Joe? We started talking about me and then you went. Was it important?'

'I'm not sure,' she said. 'That's why I wanted to ask you. You know what Max is like. And I don't want to cause trouble.'

'Fire ahead,' he said, looking more serious.

She told him about the letter and how she'd got it from Joe's room, and then about the money.

He laughed out loud. 'You little thief. If the captain hears about your escapade he'll make you walk the plank.'

She felt her colour rising. It had been a silly thing to do and now she felt even sillier standing in front of Geoffrey with him laughing at her. He saw her embarrassment and smiled. 'Nothing to worry about. Just forget about it.'

'But Joe's really concerned.'

Geoffrey shrugged. 'It goes on, Sarah. But it sounds like Kevin got a bit too greedy.'

'What, you mean it's all right?'

Geoffrey looked at her. 'Sarah, it really would be better if you didn't get involved. If you're worried, tell Max.'

She shook her head. 'I couldn't do that. It's why I wanted to ask you.'

'I can't get into it. You know I can't. It's the way business is done. Everybody knows about it. The company turns a blind eye so long as it doesn't affect the ship. But I will have a word with Joe.'

Sarah didn't know whether to be horrified or relieved. At least it didn't seem so serious now and she felt happy to let Geoffrey deal with it.

When Sarah went into the bar for a drink before lunch next day, Ben was sitting alone. Shelly took her drink from the bar and went to join him. Sebastian looked across as Shelly sat down, a smirk on his face. He picked up his drink and, walking over to them, stood looking down at Shelly. She looked up over her shoulder when she sensed he was there.

'I see our little cadet has settled for Ben after all. Safer than going after married men, sweetheart,' Sebastian said with a sneer.

Sarah heard the remark and tensed. Then she cringed as Ben shot up and grabbed Sebastian by the collar. 'What do you mean?' he growled into his face.

Sebastian drew back, then took Ben's shoulders as if to shake him off. But this only caused Ben to cling tighter.

'You take that back and apologise to her,' Ben growled.

'Jealous, are we?' Sebastian sneered,

213

holding him at a distance.

Ben took a swing with his fist and landed it straight in Sebastian's face. His glass of beer smashed on the floor and blood spurted from his nose and spattered the sleeve of his white shirt.

'You apologise to her,' Ben yelled at him.

Geoffrey and Kevin were holding Ben now as another attack became imminent, while a cold fury welled in Sebastian's eyes. He spat at Ben and walked slowly from the room, leaving the two men struggling to retain Ben.

Shelly stood a moment, shocked at the outburst, then she rushed from the room.

Sarah ran after her. When she reached her room she found Shelly slumped on her bunk in tears. She put an arm round her shoulders and tried to soothe her.

'I hate that man. He's always harassing me. He won't take no for an answer.'

Sarah tried to calm her.

'He even came to my room the other

night,' Shelly sobbed.

Sarah remembered the furtive way Sebastian had been creeping around the night she'd been in Joe's room. 'Shelly, you can't put up with this.'

Shelly stiffened. 'Sarah, don't say anything. I don't want to make a fuss.'

'But this is wrong, Shelly. You can't let it go on.'

Shelly straightened and turned a tear-stained face to her. 'I have to, Sarah. I don't want them thinking I can't stand up for myself, that I can't cope. Please don't say anything.'

'Shelly, you have to tell someone.' Her mind turned automatically to Max but she dismissed it. Max wouldn't want to know. His attitude was that if girls wanted to come to sea and live in a man's world then they had to get on with it.

Shelly took a deep breath and straightened up. 'I'm not going to let them win. I have as much right to do this job as any of them and I won't let them intimidate me.'

Sarah looked into Shelly's tear-stained face and her heart went out to her. 'I think you're so brave, Shelly. And if it's any help, I'm here for you. Come and find me at any time.'

Shelly gave a watery smile. 'Thanks, Sarah.'

* * *

'I never go ashore here,' Max told Sarah when they docked in Bangkok. 'It's all girlie bars, temples and floating markets that stink to high heaven. Wait till we get to Hong Kong. I'll take you out for one of the best meals you've ever eaten.'

'Sounds good,' she said, trying not to show disappointment that yet again he didn't seem interested in showing her around.

Shelly found Sarah after dinner and said a few of the lads were going ashore and she didn't want to be the only girl. Max seemed happy for Sarah to go with them and said he'd order a car. Shelly said it wasn't necessary as they were going to the local bar near the dock. Max frowned but put up no objection.

The bar was a dingy, poorly lit place, with girls draped on stools at the bar, dressed seductively in kimono-style dresses with flowers and other adornments in their hair. Sarah felt uncomfortable but trusted the men to keep the two of them safe. This was obviously the shadier side of Bangkok.

'What was that?' she shrieked as something small darted across the wall.

Geoffrey laughed. 'It's only a chit-chat. They're harmless.'

When she got a chance to study it more closely she saw it was a small green lizard, now sitting perfectly still, glued to the wall.

Will went up to the bar to order drinks while Geoffrey found a corner for them to sit in. Shelly was taking it all in, a look of astonishment on her face. First the girls looked at them, then turned and whispered together, then moved in on Will. He said something to them and they backed off again, giving a sour look in the direction of Shelly and Sarah.

Geoffrey noticed and was amused at Shelly's reaction. 'They don't like the competition. Does them out of business.'

'Why did you bring us here if you knew that?' Shelly asked.

He couldn't keep the smile from his face. 'Better to know what's out there when you've got a good strong escort than to walk into it unsuspecting.'

Sarah shook her head and smiled. The men had planned this to shock them and it had worked.

★ ★ ★

When she got back to the ship and told Max where they'd been he laughed. 'I could see what they were up to and I knew you'd enjoy the joke. You always want to see the place as it is. So now you have.'

'Weren't you worried about us?' Sarah said.

'Not at all. The lads knew they had to

take care of you. If any harm had come to you they'd have had me to answer to. Anyway, I know them well enough to trust them. You were quite safe.'

★   ★   ★

Next morning Sarah was up before dawn. Max had reluctantly agreed to take her to the floating market. 'What time does it start?' she asked sleepily.

'Four o'clock. But I don't think we'll quite manage that.'

Sarah didn't mind how early it was. She was excited about going and equally excited at having a day with Max away from the ship.

Slipping into a cool dress and sandals, she was ready when Max called to say the car was waiting for them. Once out of town they transferred to a small boat to navigate the narrow canals of the market.

'You look lovely,' he said, sitting opposite to her on the boat and smiling.

She yawned and smiled back. In the

hazy light of dawn she felt content to be paddled along through the murky water of the canals by the wiry old boatman.

As they drifted along it was like being transported into a bygone age. Small flat boats jockeying for position were expertly paddled by mature women who were always ready to stop and bargain. It was chaotic, noisy, colourful and fun. Long boats were piled high with tropical fruit and vegetables and strange smells drifted from floating kitchens.

Max said something to the boatman and he put out his wooden paddle towards one of the boats selling food. An old lady in a coolie hat, baggy trousers and tunic pulled them in and placed a coconut into a basket on a long pole that she extended out to their boat.

The boatman handed it to Sarah. 'Good drink.'

The coconut was full of lovely cool coconut milk which Sarah sipped through the straw, smiling gratefully at Max.

'You missed breakfast this morning. We can't have you wilting from starvation,' Max said. 'We can get off at the pier for a while and wander along the passageways if you like.'

Here the stalls were crammed together beneath brightly coloured parasols selling kaftans, fans, silks and a wonderful selection of sun hats. Sarah stopped to admire a ring with many precious stones set in the design of a Thai headdress. Max slipped it on her finger and after the usual bartering, handed over some notes. Then they sat under a parasol and ate fried bananas with coconut ice cream.

There was a stir in the crowd the other side of the square and Sarah shrieked when she saw a monkey had landed on an Indian lady's shoulder and whipped off her wig. The poor woman was distraught and the owner was trying to pacify her whilst her husband shouted abuse at him and waved a threatening hand.

'Do you want to ride the elephant?' Max gave her a roguish grin.

'No fear,' she said.

In the car on the way back to the ship

Max took her hand. 'I have enjoyed today.'

Sarah smiled. 'And to think how hard I had to work to get you to bring me.'

He gave her a whimsical smile. 'I've never enjoyed this sort of thing much. But with you it's different. You take so much enjoyment from life and I like sharing that.'

She cuddled up to him and he put an arm round her. 'Are you happy, Sarah?'

She squeezed his hand. 'I'm always happy when I'm with you.'

★　★　★

The next day he strode into the room at coffee time. 'I've done everything I have to. Would you like to go ashore for the afternoon, look round some temples if you want to?'

She stared at him. 'But you said you couldn't bear to see another temple.'

'But you would like to, wouldn't you?'

A grin began to spread across her face. 'Max, I'd love to.'

Their driver was patient, escorting them to each temple and waiting until they returned and were ready for the next one. Sarah marvelled at the splendour of each magnificent building: the Temple of the Reclining Buddha, the oldest and biggest in Bangkok, the Golden Buddha weighing five and half tons of solid gold; the Marble Temple; the Temple of Dawn on the river bank, golden against the darkening red sky; the Grand Palace, guarded with fierce stone giants, its red and gold spires reaching skyward; and finally the Emerald Buddha, carved from a solid lump of jade.

Sarah was lost in a world of splendour and colour. Red-robed monks in sandaled feet walked in groups amongst the milling throng, hot and tired and dusty. But she wouldn't have missed one minute of it. Max was beside her and she delighted in sharing the magic of the day with him.

* * *

After a cold shower, Sarah went out onto their deck, and Max put two glasses of chilled wine on the table between them. They sat watching the sun sinking low on the horizon, a great red ball turning sky and sea a molten red.

'You enjoyed today, didn't you?' Sarah said.

He nodded and gave her a fond smile. 'I always enjoy days with you.'

11

Confessions

Max raged, his face red, his fists clenched as he paced the room. Maggie sat on the settee, clutching a handkerchief and twisting it round and round in her hands as she tried to control her shaking. Sarah sat beside her, anxiously watching Max.

'You can't sail without him,' Maggie pleaded.

Sarah got up and went to Max. 'You must try to find him.'

Max walked away from her towards his desk, then turned to face her, his arms spread in front of him. 'I've done everything possible. The mate's been round every bar in the dock area. We've checked with the police, and they've checked with every hospital in Bangkok. What else can I do?'

Sarah frowned. 'We could wait till tomorrow.'

The look on his face frightened her. 'We cannot wait till tomorrow. He knew the time of departure. It's his own fault.' He banged his fist down on the desk, then walked to the door. 'We sail today.'

Maggie was in tears and Sarah tried to comfort her. 'He'll turn up. He'll be waiting for us in the next port.'

Maggie got up and began to walk unsteadily towards the door. 'I don't think so.'

Sarah took her arm and helped her back to her cabin, then returned to find Max pacing the deck. If only he would talk to her calmly instead of shouting at her and demanding he be obeyed as he was by everyone on the ship. He seemed to have forgotten she was his wife. Those moments when they would talk and she would feel close to him were becoming less frequent. Just about everything had gone wrong on this trip. So far, Max had dealt with all of it in his usual efficient manner. His chief steward deserting ship here in Bangkok was the last straw.

'I know I've done the right thing, damn it,' he growled. 'I'll arrange for them to be taken ashore.'

'What, you mean Maggie and Jess?'

'Of course I mean Maggie and Jess. I can't keep them on board for the rest of the voyage. She's been a damned nuisance since the day she arrived. That woman, with all her moaning.'

'Max, have a heart. Maggie's husband is missing. She has a right to be distraught.'

'They'll be taken care of.'

'Max, this is awful. We can't just abandon them.'

'We're not abandoning them. For goodness sake, woman, will you listen to me?'

Sarah went quiet. He'd never spoken to her like that before.

He wiped his hand across his brow and gave her a distraught look. 'Sarah, I'm sorry. Look, our agent here will look after them until the company fly them home. I can't do more than that. I'm expected to keep to a schedule. I have no choice in this. Please don't make it any harder for me.'

She went to him and took his hands in hers. 'Max, I'm sorry, too. I shouldn't interfere. You must do what you have to.'

He held her hands tightly and seemed to calm, then he left the room and she knew she wouldn't see him again until the whole thing was sorted.

She stepped onto the deck outside their room and saw Jess wandering around on the deck below. She called to her and Jess was soon sitting beside her.

'What's happening about Daddy?' Jess asked.

Sarah wanted to reassure her all would be well but she couldn't.

'Is he coming back to the ship?'

'I don't know, Jess.'

'I want him to come back. I think Mummy wants him back.'

'I'm sure she does.'

'Mummy says we might have to leave the ship here.'

'Yes, I think you will. But you'll be all right. You can stay in a nice hotel until they find Daddy and then you can all go home together.' She didn't know what else to tell her without alarming her.

'Sarah, will you come and see us when we get home?'

'I don't see how I can.'

'Why?'

'You live a long way from me, Jess.'

Jess fell silent for a moment. 'I'll never see you again, then.'

'No, I don't suppose so.'

'Why don't you have a little girl?' Jess asked her.

'That's a difficult question to answer, Jess.'

'I suppose you're like Mummy. She never wanted me.'

'Oh, Jess, that's not true. Your mother loves you.'

'I heard her telling her friend that I was a mistake.' Jess hunched her shoulders. 'She didn't know I was listening.'

Sarah took hold of Jess's hand. 'Jess, listen to me. That didn't mean she didn't want you. People say that when they haven't planned to have a baby at that time. Maybe they wanted to wait a little while.'

Jess looked at Sarah with wide-open eyes. 'I didn't know that.'

'You can't believe your mum and dad don't love you, surely.'

'No, they love me. Daddy says I'm special.' Jess's chin began to wobble and Sarah pulled her into her arms and hugged her.

'You must be patient, Jess. Mummy's had a nasty shock. You must try to help her.'

Sarah heard Max coming back into the room. 'Why don't you go down and see if Mummy's all right? If you need me, you know where I am.'

Jess jumped up and, setting her face firmly, did as she was asked.

There was a loud banging on the door and Sarah sprang up from her chair. Jess stood panting and looking very frightened. She took Sarah's hand and pulled her out of the room. 'Mummy's sick. She's gone all funny.'

Sarah tried to keep up with her as they raced along the alleyways until they got to Maggie's cabin. She was lying on the bed in her bath robe, a wet towel on her forehead, and Sarah knew she'd been drinking. There was a bottle of pain killers open on the table.

'How many of these have you taken?' Sarah asked.

Maggie gave a hollow laugh. 'Not enough, if that's what you're thinking.'

Sarah shook her. 'Maggie, I need to know.'

Maggie turned to face her. Her voice was slurred. 'Look, I have a child to look after. I know I've not been making a very good job of it lately. But she is mine. She's all I've got now. I'm not going to do anything silly, am I?' She pulled herself up and sat on the edge of the bunk, her feet dangling. 'Sarah, my life is in tatters. Kevin's left me. I need a drink to make it bearable. You surely don't begrudge me that.'

Sarah hardly knew what to say. She didn't know what had happened to Kevin or much about their relationship. 'Maggie, why don't you get yourself dressed and come down to the lounge with me?'

Maggie looked at her. 'What, and be a laughing stock? I don't think so.' Her speech was slow and her eyes not properly focusing.

'Okay, I'll make us a coffee here and we can talk.' She turned to Jess, who was watching. 'Jess, darling, will you fill the kettle, there's a good girl. I think Mummy will be fine once she's had a coffee. Then you go out on deck and time how long it takes you to walk right round the ship. I did it in ten minutes this morning. I bet you can't beat that.'

Jess frowned, then her eyes lit up. 'Bet I can.'

Maggie got off the bunk and staggered across the room. 'You surprise me, Sarah. I thought you were hard like your husband. But you're not like him at all.'

Sarah shook her head and smiled. 'Go on, get dressed. You'll feel a whole lot better then.'

As they sat together talking and drinking coffee Maggie began to buck up. 'Left me in a right mess now, he has. Not knowing where he is or if he'll turn up someday out of the blue. We've had our differences. Not much love lost between us these days. But I wasn't expecting this.'

'They're doing everything possible to trace him. Maybe he just got drunk and couldn't get back to the ship and then felt so bad he went to ground.'

Maggie huffed. 'He knew what he was doing, all right. These Malay girls, they all want to marry a white man. Think they'll take them back home. One-way ticket out of poverty. Fat chance!'

'You can't be sure of that, Maggie.'

'Oh, but I can. I found a letter in his drawer just now when I started packing. In a pink envelope. Had it all planned, he did. That money was for her. To set her up.' Maggie gave her a questioning look. 'Don't tell me you don't know what goes on. The perks they get.' Her mouth turned up in a sneer. 'Been a good voyage this time. More than usual. And there was me thinking it was for a new car.'

Sarah looked away.

'Joe's in on it as well. You ask him if you don't believe me. Nothing to me now. Kevin did the deals and now he's got the money. Can't blame me, can they?'

Sarah listened but remained silent.

'Don't know why I married him. Never been much good to me. Jess thinks the world of him. Spoils her rotten, he does. It's not right that the child has to go through all this.'

Sarah turned to her. 'Maggie, she'll be fine with you until they find him.'

Maggie straightened herself. 'Of course she will. I'm her mother, aren't I?'

Jess came running back into the room. 'I did it. Eight minutes. Do you believe me?'

Sarah smiled at her. 'Of course I do. That's very good, especially as your legs aren't as long as mine.'

'But you're much older. I suppose that's why.'

Sarah laughed. 'Okay, I'm going to leave you two now and I'll come back later if there's any news.'

She touched Maggie on the arm. 'Try not to worry. I'm sure everything will work out. We just have to give it time.'

* * *

Maggie and Jess left the ship that afternoon. Sarah helped Maggie pack while Jess sat quietly in a corner of the room. As the car drew away with them inside, Sarah waved to Jess, who bravely waved back with tears running down her face. Maggie stared blankly ahead.

Sarah stood at the top of the gangway, watching the car as it turned out of sight. And still she stood watching and waving, tears pouring down her face, her heart breaking for that little girl, until she felt familiar arms encircle her. She turned into him so that his arms could enfold and comfort her. Max was there.

* * *

Since leaving Bangkok, Max had started going up on the bridge every time Malcolm was on watch. Now he was pacing the room, up and down, up and down, until she felt dizzy watching him.

'Max, come and sit down. You'll drive me crazy if you keep this up.'

He stopped pacing and looked at her, a scowl on his face. 'I don't trust that lad. These are dangerous waters. He can't afford to stand on the bridge chatting to his wife. We don't want another incident like Penang.'

'He hasn't given you any further cause for concern, has he?'

'Once is enough, isn't it?' he growled.

'You said he deserved a second chance.'

Max glared at her. 'I'm giving him one, aren't I?'

'I think you're undermining his confidence. Anyway, Nancy wasn't even there when that happened.'

'Maybe not, but I'll swear he'd nodded off in the chartroom when he should have been keeping a lookout. He pays more attention to his wife than his job,' he growled.

'Well, nobody could accuse you of doing that.' It was out before she could stop herself. She winced when she saw the look on his face and wished with all her heart she could take the comment back. She looked up at him standing there. 'Max, I'm sorry. I should never have said that.'

He turned away from her and went to the porthole and stared out, his posture tense. His voice was low when he eventually turned and looked at her. 'No, you shouldn't.'

He began pacing again, his irritation growing. Then he turned and confronted her, his face red with anger. 'I should be able to trust my officers. This ship is my responsibility, all of it, every minute of every day. You might be on holiday but I'm not. I know what I'm doing, Sarah, and I really wish you'd accept that and not keep interfering.'

She stood up and turned away, not wanting him to see the hurt she felt at this reproach. After only a moment she felt him behind her. He took her shoulders and turned her to face him, his anger gone, his face now distorted with anguish. 'Sarah, I'm sorry. I didn't mean that. I'm stressed with all the problems on this ship. I shouldn't take it out on you. I'm sorry.' Then he turned from her, walked to his desk and slumped into the chair, leaning forward and holding his head in his hands.

She choked back a sob and went to him and put an arm round his shoulder. Her voice was tight. 'It's all right, Max. I understand. I won't interfere again.'

He didn't move.

'Max, I'm sorry. I shouldn't undermine you.' She held onto him and it seemed an age before he turned and his eyes were full of misery.

'Max, it's all right, really,' she croaked.

It took some effort for him to speak. 'No, Sarah, it isn't. I shouldn't have spoken to you like that.'

'Max, I understand.'

'No, you don't, Sarah. It shouldn't be like this.' He got up and slowly walked over and closed his door, something he rarely did. Then he took her hand and led her to the settee and sat her down beside him. She perched stiffly on the edge, wondering what it was about. She'd never seen Max like this before.

He was looking at her, tension contorting his face. 'There's something I want to tell you. I think it might help.'

Now she was really nervous. But, whatever it was, she wanted to know.

His look was far away and he swallowed. 'I can't let it happen again.'

She frowned. 'What happen again? What do you mean?'

He shook himself as if trying to bring himself back from wherever it was his mind had drifted. She swivelled off the settee and knelt on the floor in front of him, taking both of his hands in hers. 'Max, what is it? You can tell me anything. I want to know what's troubling you.'

She waited silently until he'd got himself together enough to start. The sweat was forming on his brow and he was gripping her hands, his voice hardly above a whisper. 'When I was third mate we had a collision. Another ship hit us.' He stopped. 'The captain was on the bridge at the time.' He paused again. 'He'd had too much to drink.'

She squeezed his hands in gentle encouragement for him to continue. Then it seemed to all come out in a rush. 'It was thick fog. We were sailing from Liverpool. The captain had taken over after dropping the pilot off and he asked me to check the radar. A ship came into view on the screen. I told him what I'd seen. The fog was dense. The captain should have rung for dead slow but he didn't. Then he ordered a bearing I knew would put us on a collision course with that ship. I should have stopped him.' He was shaking now and squeezing her hands so tightly it hurt.

'What happened?'

It took him some time to continue. 'I kept telling him but he ignored me and kept full speed ahead. He wouldn't listen.'

'It wasn't your fault, Max. How could it have been? You couldn't overrule the captain.'

'I should have done. I had the qualifications to take over. I knew what was about to happen. I've regretted it ever since.'

'Would he have let you?'

He seemed to be gaining control again, his voice steadying. 'I think so.

He'd asked me before when he knew he was incapable. I could have persuaded him. I could have done something. I should have. But I didn't. I just let it happen, Sarah.'

His tortured look sent a shiver of fear through her. 'Did it hit you?'

'Yes. It struck us amidships and caved in the hull. I'll never forget it: the impact, rivets cracking, plates groaning, how the ship lurched to starboard and then to port.' The sweat was pouring off him and she could hear the terror in his voice as he relived that nightmare experience. He stopped to take a breath, then rushed on. 'The shouting, everything rolling and crashing on deck, derricks bending and twisting.'

Sarah was sharing every bit of it with him. He was silent for a long time, trying to regain control. Slowly he calmed and looked up at her.

'What happened then?' she asked gently.

His voice became flat. 'Nobody was hurt. The ship was towed back to port. The captain went to pieces. He never went back to sea. He took his own life.'

Their eyes met in mutual grief.

'There was an inquest. When the facts came out they asked me why I hadn't taken over. I should have done. I could have prevented it. I've never been able to put it out of my mind. It can so easily happen.' He held his head in his hands and looked at the floor.

'But, Max, no blame was put on you, was it?'

His look was more of resignation now as he got up and began pacing the room. 'No, technically I did nothing wrong. But I knew I had. I let that man down. It ended his career. I could have prevented that. I was afraid to stand up for what I knew to be right. I've never done it since and I never will again. But I can't forget what I did then.' He stopped and looked at her. 'I've never talked about it before.'

'Max, I'm glad you told me.'

'So am I. Maybe the nightmares will go away now.'

She got up and stood in front of him.

'So you're not going to let that happen to Malcolm. Is that it?'

'Malcolm's young. He's inexperienced. But he's bright and could make a good officer. It's part of my job to make sure he does. I won't let him throw his career away as that captain did. It's something I can do to make amends.'

He stretched to his full height and went to open the door again. Sarah felt shaken but her heart was full. She was beginning to understand this complex character she had married, and the more she understood him the more she loved him.

* * *

They were on their way to Hong Kong and Max seemed calmer now. The ship had settled into its normal routine and they could spend some time together without disturbance. Sarah felt closer to him and they were more relaxed together. He wasn't going up onto the bridge as much and seemed to be allowing

Malcolm to do his watches in peace. Sarah felt the worst was behind them and that Max was back in control, of his ship and of his life.

★ ★ ★

One afternoon when Sarah was going down to the pool she saw Nancy standing with her head in her arms, leaning against the bulkhead and sobbing hysterically.

She rushed over to her. 'Nancy, what's the matter?'

Nancy just sobbed louder and twisted as if in an agony of distress.

'Nancy, talk to me. What's happened?'

Nancy turned to her, her face blotched and disfigured with grief. She was shaking and clenching and unclenching her hands against the metal. 'Malcolm told me to go down from the bridge,' she sobbed.

Sarah didn't know what to do. Nancy was in such a state.

Nancy took a deep breath. 'She's up

there with him.'

'Are you talking about Shelly?'

'Of course I am. They're up there together. And Malcolm told me to go down. She's up there on the bridge with him all the time.' She squeezed her eyes tight and held her breath until she could speak again, then turned a blotched red face to Sarah, her eyes full of misery. 'She's always with him.'

'No, Nancy, she isn't. Geoffrey spends a lot of time with her. And she's often on deck working with the bosun.'

Nancy was shaking. 'Well, every time I go up on the bridge, she's there.'

Sarah could feel Nancy's distress. 'I think it just seems that way,' she said softly.

'And she's up there with him at night,' Nancy managed through tight lips.

Sarah was trying everything she could to calm her with reason. 'Malcolm does that watch. It's all part of the job. Shelly has to do what she's told. She can't choose.'

'She's so pretty, and I think Malcolm really likes her.'

'Nancy, you're imagining things. Shelly's only interested in learning as much as she can. Why don't you talk to her? I think it would put your mind at rest.'

Nancy shook violently and Sarah took her arm but Nancy pulled away. 'He said I wasn't to go on the bridge anymore. And now Shelly's up there and I can't go up.'

Shelly appeared round the corner and stopped when she saw Nancy and Sarah, her face ashen.

Sarah looked at her. 'Shelly, what's going on?'

Shelly's chin trembled. 'Nothing. I don't know. Malcolm sent me down to look after Nancy.'

Nancy turned and stamped her feet. 'Go and get Malcolm. I want Malcolm.'

Shelly was struggling to hold back the tears, her voice shaky. 'He can't leave the bridge. He told me to come.'

'I don't want you. You're the cause of it all!' Nancy shrieked at her. 'Get Malcolm!'

Sarah turned to Shelly. 'Shelly, go and get Max.'

Shelly looked at her in horror, then burst into tears.

Sarah realised she had to get Max herself. She raced back to the room and was relieved to find him still there. 'Max, Nancy's having hysterics and she wants Malcolm and he's on the bridge.'

Max got up from his desk and left the room without a word.

Sarah rushed back to Nancy. She was shouting abuse at Shelly, who was cringing away from her. Sarah took her arm again. 'Nancy, stop it.'

Nancy turned on her, then burst into a fresh bout of sobbing. 'It's all her fault!'

Sarah was becoming angry. 'It has nothing to do with Shelly.'

'Then why do they want me out of the way?' Nancy screeched.

Malcolm came racing up the deck, went straight to Nancy and enfolded her in his arms. Gradually her sobbing subsided as Malcolm stroked her hair and spoke softly to her.

Sarah went to Shelly and put an arm round her shoulders and they stood in shock, watching Malcolm soothing Nancy. Eventually he led her away and Sarah took Shelly back to her room.

'What was all that about?' Sarah asked her gently as she sat on the bunk beside her.

Shelly was tight-lipped. 'I don't know and I don't care and I want to go home.'

'Shelly, tell me,' Sarah insisted.

Shelly's face was a picture of misery. 'He was helping me with some chart work when she came up. Malcolm said he was busy and that he'd be down soon. She burst into tears and rushed off. She's crazy.'

Sarah sighed. There was nothing more she could do. Shelly was beyond reason so she left her sitting on the bunk staring at the floor and made her way down to the pool. She needed some activity now to calm her. There was nobody else there so she swam up and down, letting the gentle rhythm of moving through the water wash away the tension. Then she got out, dried off and ambled back to her room.

Max was sitting out on deck with a gin and tonic and had already poured one for Sarah. He looked up when he heard her. 'Drinks are poured,' he said. 'Dinner in half an hour.'

'I'll just have a quick shower and change,' she called out to him.

She soon relaxed on the deck outside their room, sitting opposite to Max at the small round table. There was a slight breeze from the movement of the ship and the evening air was cooler. She picked up her glass and looked across at him. His smile was indulgent and full of love. 'Did you tell Malcolm that Nancy wasn't to go on the bridge?' she ventured cautiously.

His face clouded. 'I had a word with him, yes.'

Sarah sipped the drink. She didn't want to probe further and antagonise him again.

He frowned. 'I had to, Sarah.'

She nodded. 'I know you did.'

'Sarah, she's a nice girl, but I can't allow her to be up there all the time. She's a distraction and I have to consider Shelly, too.'

Sarah felt her heart swell with love. He wasn't a hard man. He was being fair. He was doing what he had to do.

He took her hand across the table, his eyes full of concern. 'Do you want me to have a word with Nancy?'

She smiled at him. 'If it's a kind one.'

A smile touched his lips. 'I don't think I'm very good at that. Perhaps it would be better if you did.'

He hadn't been angry. He hadn't dismissed her concern. Their eyes met and a flood of happiness swept over her.

12

A Shock for Sarah

Two days later Malcolm came looking for Sarah. 'I'm worried about Nancy. She won't come out of the room. She won't eat. She won't even talk to me. Can you try, Sarah? She might listen to you.'

Sarah shook her head. 'I doubt it. I've tried, Malcolm. She's obsessed with you and Shelly being together.'

'No, she isn't now. It's not that. We've talked it through. She knows she was wrong about that. She was upset because I asked her to go down. Max told me he didn't want her up there all the time. I didn't have a choice.'

'Maybe you didn't do it very tactfully,' Sarah said.

He looked sheepish. 'That's what upset her. But we're all right again now.'

Sarah sighed. 'What, then?'

'She feels embarrassed. She can't face anyone. But she can't stay in the room for the rest of the voyage. Please, Sarah.'

'But why would she listen to me? She doesn't seem to want to talk to anyone except you.'

From the look he gave her it seemed he was reluctant to say more and she felt a stab of remorse that she was being so unsympathetic. Then he seemed to make the decision to go on, but his tone was measured now as if he was thinking carefully before he spoke.

'She's easily intimidated, Sarah. Last voyage the captain's wife was one of those self-important people and she put Nancy down a few times.'

'But I'm not like that.' Sarah was horrified.

He was quick to defend himself. 'No, you're not. That's why I want you to talk to her.'

'Is she always like this with people she doesn't know?'

He shook his head. 'Depends on the people. She was training to be a nurse when we met. The patients loved her. She's very gentle and kind.'

'So she gave it up to be with you?' Sarah asked.

'I didn't want her to. I mean, I wanted her with me, but it's a big thing to give up your career, especially one you love.'

'Did you talk to her about it?'

'Yes, but she'd made up her mind.'

Sarah was beginning to see a different Nancy. 'I'll talk to her, Malcolm. I won't promise anything, but I'll try.'

'Thanks, Sarah.'

★   ★   ★

Sarah was more worried about Shelly. She'd been withdrawn and moody since the incident, going about her work in silence and avoiding everyone. When Sarah had tried to talk to her she'd blanked her out and walked away. Ben was worried, too. He'd spoken to Sarah about it and it seemed he was the only one who Shelly would talk to. But Ben felt he wasn't getting through to her and was worried about what to do.

When Sarah got to Nancy's room, Shelly was coming out. She walked past Sarah, not even looking at her. Nancy was sitting on the bunk, hands clasped, staring at the floor.

Sarah sat beside her. 'What's going on, Nancy?'

Nancy looked at her. Her voice was calm and quiet. 'I'm stupid and pathetic.'

'What did Shelly say? I saw her coming out.'

'She said she didn't know what she'd done to upset me but whatever it was she wanted to try to put it right.'

'See, I told you. I hope you two can be friends now.'

'That's what she said.' Her voice was expressionless.

'And will you?'

Nancy stiffened. 'I don't know if I can. What must everyone be thinking of me?'

Sarah put an arm round her shoulder

and she didn't flinch.

'I can't face them.'

Sarah squeezed her shoulders. 'Shelly doesn't have that luxury. She has to get on with it, carry on working, face up to everyone. I think you should support her.'

Nancy frowned, then looked away. 'I don't know if I can.'

*　*　*

Shelly was in overalls, staining the teakwood deck. She drew a hand across her forehead and pushed a strand of hair out of her eyes.

'That looks like hot work,' Sarah said as she approached her.

Shelly shrugged. 'Got to be done.'

'I've been talking to Nancy. She's really sorry about what happened.'

Shelly carried on with her work in silence.

'She's really embarrassed about the whole thing.'

'Good,' Shelly said with feeling.

'Shelly, that's not like you.'

Shelly stopped what she was doing and looked at Sarah. 'Look, I haven't caused any of this. I do what I'm told. I don't make a fuss. And now I want you to leave me alone to get on.' She turned back to the section of deck she was working on and gave it her all.

Sarah was shocked at the outburst and decided she was having nothing more to do with either of them.

★ ★ ★

They sailed into Victoria Harbour under azure skies and a flat sea. Sarah stood beside Max on the bridge with the pilot and watched huge cargo ships manoeuvring in and out of the port. The Hong Kong shoreline was a mass of towering buildings. Ferry boats plied across the harbour between the mainland and the island. A fire boat carrying out its safety checks could be seen spraying an arc of water high into the air. On every side there was activity, something of interest to watch. Sarah felt her heart quicken. She couldn't wait to get ashore with Max.

Once they docked Max disappeared as usual, but when he eventually came back he told her he'd organised a car to take her into the town with Nancy. 'You can shop to your heart's content.'

Her face fell.

'I thought you'd enjoy that.' Max gave her a perplexed look.

'Not today, Max. I wanted us to go ashore together.'

'Sarah, I can't leave the ship today. Joe's accident and Kevin going missing have created a load of work for me. There are endless documents to produce for Immigration and reports to write for the company. You go and enjoy yourself with Nancy and I'll try to get away tomorrow.'

She was determined to be more understanding and let him get on with his business in peace, but she didn't relish a day with Nancy. Would Nancy really want to go shopping with her?

She hadn't seen her since leaving her room the other day.

Nancy was at the top of the gangway looking cool and composed in a simple linen shift dress and sandals when Sarah joined her.

'I'm sorry if Max talked you into this,' Sarah said. 'He does tend to assume things.'

Nancy gave her a shy smile. 'It was my idea, actually.'

Sarah was astounded. 'Was it?'

'I was trying to find you to ask if you'd come ashore with me and I bumped into Max.'

'What did he say?' Sarah still couldn't believe what she was hearing.

'He very kindly said he would arrange a car for us.'

Sarah smothered a snort and stopped herself saying I bet he did.

Nancy looked apprehensive. 'I hope you don't mind. I really wanted to ask you myself.'

'Of course not. I'm glad of the company.' Sarah said, as they walked down the gangway. She didn't want to make a big deal of it in case she frightened Nancy off again.

Enormous blocks of flats rose on either side as the car eased its way through the traffic. Poles of washing protruded like horns from windows, and there were strange smells of cooking and exhaust fumes and poor sanitation. A man in baggy trousers and a straw hat pushed a cart. Down little side streets small shops spilled their goods onto the pavement amongst the throng of shoppers.

When the taxi dropped them off in the middle of a bazaar, Nancy stood looking perplexed. Sarah took her arm and guided her across the busy road towards one of the side streets. 'We'll miss Maggie bartering for us.'

Nancy looked at her. 'I rather prefer it without her. She was a bit overpowering.'

Sarah giggled and Nancy managed a smile.

As they meandered along the busy

street looking at the merchandise, Nancy picked up a rosewood carving of an old man reading a book. 'Isn't he beautiful?'

'Get him, then,' Sarah encouraged.

'I'm not sure Malcolm would like him.'

'Oh, get him anyway. I'm sure he'll come to love him.' Sarah nudged her and they both giggled as Nancy got out her purse.

Sitting in the sun over tea and cakes and watching other shoppers, they talked easily. The more Sarah got to know Nancy, the more she liked her and enjoyed her company.

Nancy's expression changed and she picked up her fork and began to turn it over and over. 'I spoke to Shelly.'

Sarah's heart missed a beat. Not more trouble, she hoped.

'I told her I was sorry and that I'd like us to be friends.' She paused.

'And?'

'And she was really good about it. We're okay now. I wish I hadn't been so stupid.'

Sarah breathed again. 'That's great, then.'

'You've helped me a lot. I wouldn't have done it if you hadn't made me see how difficult it was for Shelly. I always thought she was so confident. But she's had a rough time, too. We're going to try to support each other now.'

Sarah shook her head and smiled. 'You two needed your heads banging together.'

Nancy looked alarmed, then smiled. 'I'm glad we fixed it before you did that.'

They both laughed and Sarah felt at last peace would reign.

★ ★ ★

When she got back on board Geoffrey was coming out of their room and he side-stepped her and didn't say a word; didn't even look at her. Max had a grim look on his face.

'What's happened?' she asked.

Max went to his desk and gathered

some papers into a bunch and put them in the drawer. 'It's no concern of yours, my dear.' Then he turned to her and forced a smile. 'Now, tell me, have you had a good day?'

Sarah worried he'd got wind of her involvement with Joe. Or maybe he suspected that she and Geoffrey were getting a bit too close. Something wasn't right. But she knew she wouldn't get anywhere by insisting he told her. She'd just have to wait until she saw Geoffrey.

★ ★ ★

The chance arose the next day when she found him alone in the ship's office.

'You looked very serious the other day when I saw you coming out of our room.'

Geoffrey looked up from the desk with a puzzled expression, then seemed to remember. 'Oh, yesterday. No, just something I had to discuss with Max. Nothing for you to worry about.'

She tensed.

'Sarah, you know I can't discuss ship's business with you.'

Geoffrey was right. But she had to know if it had anything to do with her. If it did, she wanted a chance to explain to Max.

'It's not about us, is it?' she ventured.

He shook his head and smiled. 'No.'

'Joe's not in trouble, is he?'

Geoffrey sighed. 'It's more serious than I thought.'

She winced and swallowed. 'Did my name crop up?'

'No, and I told Joe not to let it.'

'Is Joe in big trouble?'

'Sarah!' His voice took on a threatening tone.

She swallowed to force down the hurt.

When he spoke again his voice was gentle. 'Max will deal with it. He'll talk to Joe, put him straight.' Then he relaxed and his eyes told her he understood her concern. 'Joe will be okay. Max is going to put him in charge in Kevin's place.

He wants Joe to clean things up and get his self-respect back. You know, Sarah, I shouldn't be discussing this with you.'

'I'm sorry, Geoffrey. I was worried about Joe, that's all. I won't make trouble.'

'I know you won't. But you have to stop worrying. Max has everything under control. He was on to it long before I went to see him.' He shook his head and smiled at her. 'Now, how about Nancy? You two seem to be getting on well.'

'She's fine now. Had a bit of a blip, that's all. And thanks, Geoffrey.'

'Glad I can help,' he said, and he returned to the lists he was studying.

* * *

Next morning while Sarah and Max were having coffee in their room, there was a knock at the door. Ben popped his head round and Sarah couldn't help noticing how much he had changed from the timid little cadet who'd joined the ship in Liverpool all those weeks ago. He was a confident young man now. His spots had cleared and the sun had given him some colour and bleached his hair golden.

'A few of us are going up Victoria Peak this afternoon,' he said. 'Would you and Sarah like to come, sir?

'Sarah will go.' Max said. 'I'll stay behind. Tell the mate I want him on board.'

Ben frowned. 'Sir, the second mate has offered to stay behind. We had persuaded the mate to come with us. He's been a bit down since his little boy was ill. We thought it would cheer him up.'

Max glared at Ben. 'Tell the mate I want him on board.'

Ben lowered his eyes. 'Yes, sir.' He went out quietly.

Sarah turned to Max. 'Why did you do that? I think it was very kind of Ben.'

'I want my chief officer on board.'

She sighed and went into the bedroom to gather her things together for the outing. A few minutes later she heard the door close and she knew he'd left the room. She sat on the edge of the bed and stared at the floor. She didn't want to go on the trip now. All the excitement had gone out of it. She'd interfered again and annoyed Max.

She changed her dress and shoes and brushed her hair. Her face in the mirror looked small and tense. Even through her newly acquired tan the paleness showed. Despondently, she walked to the top of the gangway and waited for the others to come.

Ben came striding along the deck with Shelly close behind him. She looked bright and happy in an orange flared dress and seemed back to her normal good humour. Nancy appeared in a cream cotton dress that flared gently over her knees, elegant as always. Sebastian was close behind.

They started to file down the gangway. At the bottom Sarah looked up. Geoffrey was sauntering down dressed in shorts and polo shirt and he smiled when he caught her eye.

They walked along the quay together. 'I didn't think you were coming,' Sarah said.

'Nearly didn't. First Ben tells me I'm to stay on board. Captain's orders. Then Max tells me to get off and enjoy myself. I didn't even want to come in the first place.' He smiled. 'I'm glad I have now, though.'

They swarmed onto the ferry and Sarah felt her heart lighten. Geoffrey could smile at troubles and they melted.

The ancient funicular tram carried them up the peak and, as Geoffrey leant over to look out at the view, the touch of his bare arm against Sarah's sent a tremble of desire through her. She was acutely aware of his spicy freshness, the golden hairs on his arms and the warmth of his body.

Their eyes met and her desire deepened. She struggled to fight it. If only Max were here. If only he didn't keep pushing her away. Geoffrey shifted slightly in his seat and the pressure of his arm against hers almost made her groan. She felt trapped. She loved Max. She wanted him beside her. But he didn't seem to feel the same. He preferred to stay on his ship. Geoffrey moved his leg and it touched hers and a shiver prickled her skin. She leant into him and closed her eyes and wished she could stay like this forever. What was happening to her?

When they got out at the top she felt sure everyone could read her thoughts and feelings like a book. She tried to act normally and talk in a normal voice but it sounded strained. Geoffrey got them a coffee in the café and Nancy came over and sat beside her. The effort of talking to Nancy calmed her and gradually she recovered her equilibrium and looked around for some distraction. Sebastian was eyeing Shelly as she sat talking to Ben at a nearby table.

Geoffrey had seen it, too. He glanced at Sarah. 'I think Sebastian fancies her, you know.' He shook his head. 'There's trouble brewing there.'

Sebastian walked over to Shelly. He put a hand on her back as he bent down with his face close to her ear. Shelly jumped up and faced him. There was an angry exchange. Sarah was on her feet. Geoffrey stopped her. Nancy let out a gasp.

'But he's upset her,' Sarah protested.

Ben was at her side and Sebastian gave him a withering look and walked away.

Sarah sat down again.

'It's okay. Let Ben sort it,' Geoffrey said.

'Yes, you're right. He'll look after her.'

Nancy went and sat beside Shelly and they began to talk quietly while Ben looked on.

'Well, who would have believed that? Our Nancy's really come out of her shell,' Geoffrey said. Then he got up. 'Let's go for a walk. I need a break from all this hassle.'

Sarah couldn't think of any excuse

not to, so she followed him towards the path leading round the peak. The panoramic view stretched across skyscrapers, to the harbour and then to the islands beyond, with ferry boats steaming their way between the island and the mainland. The path led through wooded areas and in parts they could see right across the island from rocky mountains to green fertility.

'It's lovely up here,' Sarah said. 'So quiet and fresh. It's like escaping from reality.'

'Do you want to escape, Sarah?'

Sarah stopped and turned to him. 'I do today. I don't know where I am with Max. Sometimes I feel he really doesn't need me at all.'

'You know Louise has only written three letters to me this voyage.'

'Geoffrey, you have to give her a chance. Wait till you get home. It will seem different then. You can talk it over.'

'I don't think there's anything to talk over. I think she's made up her mind.'

'How do you feel about it?' she asked.

'I don't know.' He gave her a wan smile. 'We're both in the same boat, you and me, aren't we?'

She wanted him to enfold her in his arms and make the hurt go away. 'I do love Max. I wish I knew he felt the same. But I don't. I sometimes think he'd rather go back to his bachelor life and be free to roam the seas without any encumbrance.'

Geoffrey looked away into the distance, them back at her. 'I love Louise, too. We used to be good together. When we had problems, we could talk about them. But she's changed. I don't know where I am with her anymore.'

'She's probably feeling lonely and stressed. It can't be easy bringing up little ones on your own, especially when they get ill.'

'That's the problem. But it's one I can't do anything about.'

He took her in his arms and held her close and she relaxed against him, knowing he needed the comfort as much as she did.

* * *

Shelly was very quiet on the way home. Sarah caught up with her as they boarded the ship.

'Sarah, he was out of order.'

'What did he say?'

'I'm not repeating it. Ben said I ought to report him. But I couldn't. It's too embarrassing.'

'Shelly, you have to if he's really harassing you. Max would deal with him.'

'No, I have to deal with it myself. But I think he's worried because Ben heard him. He probably thinks I'll make a fuss about it and get him into trouble.'

Sarah admired her strength. She had to let her cope with it in her own way and she wasn't at all sure Max would be sympathetic. At least Shelly had Ben to look out for her.

* * *

Sarah was looking forward to the promised visit to Max's Chinese friends on the island. She loved sharing this side of his life with him, meeting friends she'd only heard about. And this family had two young children, which made it more of a treat.

'We must take them presents,' Sarah said the morning they were due to go.

'No point,' Max said. 'I did that once and Cheng said they didn't have time to play. They were too busy studying. So I took them back home for my nephews.'

'But I thought you said they were small boys.'

'Sarah, wait till you see their apartment. It's not like ours, you know.'

Together with George, they caught the ferry across from Kowloon to the island. Cheng was there to meet them and, as they made their way up the tower block where he lived, Sarah felt they must be perched in the sky.

The flat was tiny, just one room with

a small recess for a kitchen. All the walls had bunk beds lined up against them. Several women were preparing food and Sarah marvelled at how so many women could fit into such a small space. They smiled shyly at her and made a big fuss of Max and George. The two little boys stared at Sarah. She spoke to them and received a very polite answer in very correct English as Cheng looked on with pride.

The four of them sat at the table in the centre of the room and Cheng poured drinks. Sarah thought it odd that the women kept bringing in dishes of food but didn't join them to eat. It wasn't until they'd eaten all they could that the women and boys came to the table and ate what was left.

The two boys were soon on the floor playing with some dice. Sarah itched to be down there with them and finally couldn't resist. Cheng looked pleased and told them to show Sarah what the game was about. The boys seemed amused that she was playing with them and took great delight in showing her what to do. Soon she was lost in the game.

Max watched as she tossed the dice. The boys had their eyes glued on it. Sarah had a low score. They let out a whoop and Sarah pulled a face, pretending disappointment. They gave her the dice again and insisted she have another go. They couldn't bear to see her sad. Max watched. She had that effect on children. They loved her. Again his conscience pricked. But he couldn't do it. He would do anything for Sarah, but not this. He simply couldn't take that risk. But was he being fair to her? Should he have married her when he knew this? Would it be kinder to set her free, let her find fulfilment with someone who could make her truly happy?

As she got up, she turned and saw Max looking at her. Conversation was going on all round him but he was in his own thoughts and the anguish in his face made her heart twist. She caught his eye and he gave her a weak smile, then looked away.

They said little on the way back. Max seemed subdued and Sarah knew it had something to do with the look he'd given her. They responded to George's banter but only in a half-hearted way until in the end he gave up.

She was tempted to broach the subject when they got back. Could Max be weakening? He did seem to get on well with Jess. She felt some hope. But as usual he disappeared and she didn't see him again until dinnertime. It was later that evening before she felt she had him to herself. After gearing herself up all evening, she still felt nervous about approaching the subject.

He was in his desk chair looking morose, and she was having difficulty getting him into conversation at all. She perched on the edge of the settee to face him, determined to get to the bottom of what was on his mind. 'They were such a lovely family. The children were a delight.'

He nodded his agreement.

'They all seemed happy together, and Cheng is so proud of his boys.'

'I knew you'd enjoy it,' he said in a matter-of-fact tone.

She took a deep breath. 'I do miss Jess.'

He nodded. 'Yes, Jess was an unusually bright child.'

'You got on well with Jess, didn't you? I know she really enjoyed the times you spent with her.' She knew she was pushing her luck but now she'd started she wasn't going to give up.

He was becoming irritated, she could tell, and yet something inside her wouldn't let the subject go. 'You'd make a lovely dad, you know.' She'd said it now and there was no taking it back.

He gave a loud sigh. 'Sarah, I know where this is leading and I don't want to go there.'

The measured tone of his voice silenced her, but she was aching with loneliness and her chin began to tremble. He was cutting her off again, not even prepared to share her innermost grief, the unbearable longing that was at her essence.

The cold anger as his eyes held hers was changing and an anguished look touched his mouth. 'Sarah, I can't do it.'

Suddenly he swung round in his swivel chair and pressed his hands each side of his head. She watched in shock for a moment, then went to him and, putting her arm round him, leant into his shoulder and let the tears come. The closeness and tears released the tension inside her as she clung to him. Eventually he pulled himself up and turned to her, his face distraught. He pushed himself up from his chair, leaning heavily on the desk. She moved back as he took her arms and put a distance between them. After looking deeply into her eyes he turned and walked unsteadily to the side of the room and stared out of the porthole. 'I can't take that risk.'

'What risk?' Her heart was thumping. She felt fear and anguish as she watched him. He was more in control now but she could see the effort it was taking. 'Max, talk to me.' She went to him and put a hand on his arm. 'Max, what are you afraid of? You have to tell me.'

There was a long pause, then his face took on a resigned look and he took her hand. 'Come and sit down.' He perched beside her on the settee, still gripping her hand, and the way he was looking into her eyes with such intensity frightened her.

'Max, what is it?'

He swallowed and his voice came out as a croak. 'It's something that happened a long time ago.'

'Max, what?'

He was gearing himself up for something difficult. 'I can't keep it to myself any longer. You have a right to know.'

She squeezed his hand in encouragement.

He opened his mouth but no sound came. He cleared his throat and drew his hand across his hair. Then he began again. 'My aunt died in childbirth. The baby died, too.'

Sarah felt the blood drain from her. This was the reason. And he'd never said. She hardly knew anything about his family.

'I was young at the time but I remember the atmosphere in the house. I shall never forget. It seemed to go on for ever. My mother and father would talk quietly about it, thinking I wasn't listening. Then there'd be long silences and tears. I don't think my mother ever got over it. She never had any more children herself.' His voice was so quiet it was almost impossible to make out the words.

He was looking at her, his expression tortured. She gently drew him to her. 'Max, things are different now.'

'I know.' The expression on his face told her how much mental anguish the memory had caused him.

'But Max, I'm fit and well.'

He shook his head. 'I've told myself that a million times. But it's no good. I can't do it.'

She felt her heart sink. She had been so sure he was changing his mind.

He was becoming agitated. 'If anything went wrong, I might be the other side of the world. I wouldn't be there to care for you. I couldn't do that. I love you too much.' The intensity in his voice made her heart contract.

She was willing the tears not to spill out. 'Max, it's all right. I understand. We don't have to. We have each other. It's enough.'

He sat very still and his voice was little more than a whisper. 'But it's not enough, is it? It's not enough for you.' He turned away from her. 'I wish I'd realised that before I asked you to marry me.'

Her heart stopped. 'What do you mean?'

His eyes met hers. 'I mean that I can never give you what you most want.' He got up and looked at his watch. 'I have to go up on the bridge. We're due to sail.'

She felt paralysed with shock and fear as she watched him walk from the room with tears pouring down her face. She didn't go up on the bridge as she usually did when they were sailing from a port. Her mind was in turmoil. What had he meant? The more she thought about it the more troubled she became.

It was after midnight when he came back. She didn't move but let him slide into bed beside her. She was too exhausted to talk anymore and she knew he would be, too.

But Max didn't sleep. All the time he'd been on the bridge his mind had gone over and over it and still he couldn't come to a decision. He knew Sarah was spending time with Geoffrey. He was a very plausible young man and Max could see the attraction. Sarah was young, full of life, full of adventure. She was compassionate and caring. She should have married someone like

Geoffrey. Did she feel trapped in their childless marriage? Was he being fair in keeping her tied to him when she so obviously needed more than he could give to make her truly happy?

13

Shelly in Danger

The subject of children didn't crop up again and Sarah knew it wouldn't. Max had given his reasons and that was it. He never went in for lengthy discussions. But he did seem more subdued, quieter than usual, and she would often catch him deep in thought.

She hadn't been able to face the reality of what he'd implied and had tried to put it out of her mind. But the more she thought about it the more she realised it was up to her to resolve the issue. She'd accepted long ago that there would be no children in their marriage. She should never have forced the subject on him again. However unbelievable it might seem to her that anyone could feel the way Max did, the fear was very real for him. Pursuing it could only drive him into feeling more inadequate and push them further apart.

What she had to do was convince him that it didn't matter, that she accepted it. Then they could get back to where they were. Telling him wouldn't work. She had to show him that having each other was all that mattered and prove to him how much she loved him.

Slowly the tension between them eased and she tried to persuade herself that they had faced a huge hurdle and come through stronger than ever. But there were moments when it was more difficult to do. The way he looked at her sometimes, the quiet moments when he'd seem deep in thought — there was still something not quite right.

*　*　*

The ship was approaching Borneo and Sarah was up on the bridge with Max when Malcolm came through from the chartroom. 'Hi, Sarah. Going ashore?

We thought we'd hire a speed boat and go up the Rajang River.'

Max was beside the helmsman, taking the ship into port. He looked round. 'We'll all go. Good day out. Should be tied up by midday. I'll get the agent to lay on a boat for us. The girls will enjoy it.'

Sarah's heart did a little skip. Max was back to his old self again. And he was making an effort to please her. He wanted to be with her. They were to have a whole afternoon with no ship coming between them.

Once they'd anchored she went down from the bridge to change for the outing. It was a beautiful day, the sun hot, the sky a perfect blue, so she decided to walk round the deck first. Shelly was up on the foc'sle checking the anchor cable. As they chatted, Nancy came along.

'Shelly, I've been looking for you. The boat's due in an hour. Joe's packed loads of food for us. We'll see you down by the pilot ladder at two.'

Eventually Max escaped the constant demands of the ship and made it up to the room. He quickly changed out of his uniform and they went down to join the others.

★   ★   ★

Max looked a little anxious as Malcolm took the helm and the small motorboat bounced across the water, dodging driftwood and logs floating in the river. He put his arm round Sarah's shoulders and she snuggled closer. Tropical jungle lined the banks, the sky was unbelievably blue, and she and Max were all right again.

Ben put his arm round the back of Shelly's seat. Shelly rested her head on his shoulder and his arm tightened round her. Sarah smiled and felt a warm glow. Such a little gesture, meaning so much.

They reached a tiny village flanked by jungle and tied the boat up at an old wooden jetty. Children jabbered in

Malay. A small boy with bare feet ran up to them and held out his hand. Malcolm ignored him, but Ben gave him a dollar.

They sat at a table outside a warehouse stacked with sacks of peppercorns and were served ice-cold beer by an old woman in a long black skirt, her face and hands wrinkled like brown leather. The afternoon sun was fierce. Hens clucked around their feet in the dirt. Some boys were kicking a rattan ball around. Max seemed relaxed and Sarah loved it all: the peace, the simplicity, even the smells of rotten food and poor sanitation.

'Let's find a spot for our picnic,' Malcolm said. 'Preferably where we can breathe fresh air.'

Max let him take over as they got the food from the boat and walked along a path by the river until they found a small clearing among the mangroves and palms. After they'd eaten, Nancy and Malcolm disappeared along the path. Ben was leaning on his elbow, stretched out on a piece of the canvas they'd brought to protect them from the damp ground, plucking at a leafy branch he'd pulled from a bush. He looked at Shelly, his eyes meeting hers and holding them with a new confidence. He got up, walked over to the bank and stood with his hands in his pockets, staring out across the river. Shelly watched him for a few moments, then got up and walked over to join him, slipping her arm through his and looking with him out over the water. Sarah leant against Max and closed her eyes, content just to be there with him.

When Nancy and Malcolm came back, Shelly and Ben were sitting together holding hands and smiling at each other. Nancy nudged Malcolm and a knowing look passed between them.

Shelly seemed glowing with happiness as, hand in hand, she and Ben followed Malcolm and Nancy back to the boat. Ben looked different. The tension had gone and his eyes were smiling, those lovely blue eyes in that tanned face. Sarah had never seen Ben look like this before. All the way back in the boat he seemed on top of the world and Sarah was happy for them.

★　★　★

As they relaxed over a drink on deck before dinner, Sarah watched Max from her deckchair where he stood at the rail looking out over the water. He turned and she smiled at him. 'I enjoyed today.'

He returned the smile. 'I wanted you to.'

'Are we all right again, Max?' Her heart was thumping.

The smile left his face but his eyes were full of love. 'I hope so.'

★　★　★

When they docked in Singapore, homeward bound, Max was instantly in demand. There were phone calls to and from head office deciding whether a replacement for Kevin was necessary or whether Joe could take over temporarily. The stores declaration needed to be checked and there was a stevedore wanting to see him about some cargo. Sarah resigned herself to a morning reading her book.

Mid-morning he strode into the room. 'All done. Get your glad rags on. We are going ashore.'

She stared at him. 'Where?'

'I've finished all I have to do. The mate can do the rest. Today I am taking my wife for a very special treat. I intend to take you to the best hotel in Singapore.'

She looked at him and there was a hint of disbelief in her voice. 'You don't mean Raffles?'

'I do. So put something nice on. I just have to take these papers to the radio officer and check the stores with Joe, then I'm all yours.'

* * *

As they drove through the town her excitement grew. Max looked smart in a well-cut linen jacket and trousers with a pale blue shirt that emphasised his healthy tanned skin and dark eyes. She looked at him sitting there beside her in the car and felt a glow of pride. She was here with her husband who was taking her to lunch in what was probably the most famous hotel in the world, and she felt the luckiest girl alive.

The car swept into the hotel grounds and came to a halt in front of its impressive colonial façade, white columns, red tiled roof and marble steps. They were welcomed by one of the famous Indian doormen, resplendent in turban, baggy trousers and gold braided white tunic. He gave a respectful nod as they walked up the steps and Max acknowledged him with a smile.

Sarah was speechless at the sheer opulence of the front entrance hall with its candelabras and rich oriental carpets. It screamed old world charm and colonial splendour. As they proceeded through the building along cool arched walkways, she glimpsed a tea garden set beneath shady palms. The sky was a clear crystal blue, the sun dazzling the white columns and arched windows. Max seemed in no hurry. He was enjoying showing her around a place he knew well, impressing her with all its splendour, and she was happy to stroll with him, enjoying the closeness they shared.

In the Long Bar she was transported back in time amidst the dark carved wood and subtle lighting. Punnka fans kept the air cool and Max found them a table near one of the windows. A waiter was instantly at their side and Max asked for Singapore slings.

'Frothy red cocktails,' he laughed. 'Made with gin and brandy. Raffles invented them.'

She watched the barman mix and shake the cocktail with crushed ice, then strain it and top the crystal goblets with cherries and pineapple. It wasn't what Max would normally drink but he was indulging her and she was lapping it up.

They sat facing each other at the small table overlooking the gardens and, as he chatted with the barman, she saw how at home he was in a place like this, a place she could only have dreamed of. He was a true man of the world with his cultured voice and his faultless manners. His toned muscles showed beneath the fine linen of his well-cut shirt. Years spent in the tropics had left him with a permanent tan and he had the bearing of a man who was always in command. His short hair was ruffled slightly from the breeze wafting in from the gardens surrounding the hotel, and a great surge of emotion took her back all those years ago when she had first fallen in love with him.

When the waiter walked away, Max turned his dark eyes on her and watched indulgently as she sipped the cocktail and rolled her eyes in pleasure. His eyes told her he was enjoying this day away from the ship and all the responsibility to be just with her. This was the Max she knew and loved.

They dined on lobster as waiters in tall hats hovered. Max never took his eyes off her. After lunch they strolled through cool arched walkways overlooking pristine lawns set with palms beneath an azure sky. In the shopping arcade Max picked up a necklace and fastened it round her neck. It was studded with small diamonds and rubies. She looked in the mirror and loved it. He paid the pretty Chinese assistant and refused to have it wrapped. 'I want you to wear it,' he told Sarah. 'To remember how happy we were today.' He put an arm round her shoulder. 'And to remind you of how much I love you.'

She put her hand to her throat and touched the necklace. So long as she had Max's love she could face anything.

* * *

'You look so much better, Joe,' Sarah said when he appeared with coffee next day.

He placed the tray on the table in

front of her. 'I'm fine now. Had another letter from Jen. She's out of hospital and sounded really excited. I hope nothing goes wrong, Sarah. I really want this baby.'

She put down her book. 'Joe, I told you not to read too much into that letter.'

He smiled. 'Homeward bound. Not long now.' Then he looked more serious. 'I told Max about the money.'

'What did he say?'

'He was really good about it. He's put me in charge now till we get back to Liverpool, so I can put a stop to it.'

'And will you, Joe?'

'Of course I will. I always knew it was wrong. I'll never get involved in anything like that again.'

'I know you won't, Joe. You're a good man.'

He grinned at her. 'Thanks, Sarah, for everything.'

★ ★ ★

Shelly was walking round the hatches, making her nightly check that the covers were secure. It was a beautiful moonlit night, the lights of the port reflecting on the water thrilling her as it always did. She was right at the stern and everything was quiet; no cargo work tonight. There was hardly anyone on board. They were all having a last fling in Singapore before the long sea voyage home.

Suddenly a hand came over her mouth from behind. It twisted her round and roughly pinned her against the hatch. She felt her back hurt and looked up into the leering face of Sebastian. He'd been drinking and was breathing heavily. She opened her mouth to scream, but his hand covered it. She pushed, but her slight strength was no match for his.

'Now, sweetheart, let's stop playing games shall we?' His sneering face was close to hers and the smell of cigars and whisky nauseated her.

He laughed. 'Flirting with the others. Trying to make me jealous. Then when

I come looking for you, what do I get? Not a very warm welcome, do I? You really shouldn't lead a man on like that you know.'

She squirmed to free herself and his grip tightened. 'Not so much of a hurry. I've seen you with Ben and Will. And then there's Malcolm.'

She twisted her head away from his hand.

'You really shouldn't mess with married men you know.'

She struggled to free herself from his iron grip but couldn't move. 'Get off me or I'll scream.'

'You know, you're much prettier when you're angry. You scream all you like, darling. Nobody will hear you at this distance. Anyway, they're all ashore or asleep. You're all mine tonight. So where shall we go to continue in a bit more privacy?'

Fear was taking over from anger now as she realised his strength was way beyond anything she could overcome and that the ship was almost deserted and probably nobody would hear her.

'Malcolm will hear me. He's checking the gangway.'

'I think you'll find Malcolm has other things on his mind.'

She was rigid with fear as he started to pull at the buttons of her shirt, his smooth hands groping her. His face came close to hers and she turned her head away.

'And you better tell that boyfriend of yours to keep his mouth shut. We don't want any nasty accidents, do we?'

His hand tightened round her arm. Her mind wouldn't work. What had she been told? Kick where it hurts. That was it. With all her strength she brought her knee right into his groin and he fell backwards with a yell over one of the securing ropes, sprawling on the deck. She was round the hatch and along the deck to the ladder before he recovered. Once in her room she slammed the door and locked it.

She couldn't stop shaking. She sat on the edge of her bunk in her tiny cabin and stared at the wall, a mixture of helpless frustration and anger churning her insides. She should be safe on a ship. She'd learned to cope with the teasing and the patronising. But not this.

Half an hour later there was a knock at her door and when she didn't answer she heard Malcolm calling her name. Then he tried to open it. 'Shelly, are you in there?'

Slowly she moved to unlock it and allow him in. He looked at her tear-stained face and froze. 'Shelly what's wrong? Why didn't you report back to me?'

Blankly she told him.

'My god, I'll kill him,' he said.

'Please don't say anything, Malcolm,' she begged.

'Don't say anything? Why?' He was outraged.

Tears poured down her face. 'I don't want to cause a fuss. Everyone will think it was my fault, that I asked for it. You know what they're like on this ship.'

Malcolm shook his head. 'I'm going to get Nancy.'

Nancy came down with a glass of brandy, which she forced Shelly to drink. Then she perched on the bunk beside her and held her hand. She didn't ask any questions, but waited for Shelly to speak.

'He came to my room the other night,' Shelly said.

'What happened?' Nancy asked softly.

'I slammed the door in his face. I think that's what upset him. He's not used to taking no for an answer.'

'He's a monster,' Nancy said. 'You have to report him, Shelly. Really, you do.'

Shelly sat rigid. 'I'm okay now, Nancy. I need to finish my rounds, then get some sleep. And thanks for coming.'

'Malcolm said he'd see to all that. You stay here and get some rest. And if you're worried in the night just come and knock on our door. Promise?'

Shelly gave her a watery smile. 'Promise.'

Sarah had found out from Nancy about what had happened and had been sworn to secrecy. She wasn't happy about not telling Max but felt obliged to keep the confidence. Sarah pondered all day about what she should do. If he'd got away with it once, what was to stop him molesting her again?

They were sitting out on deck that evening, enjoying the sunset before going down to dinner. 'I haven't seen Sebastian today. Is he all right? He's always out on deck in the afternoon,' Sarah said, edging round the subject.

Max frowned. 'Not missing his company, are you?'

'Not at all. He's a horrible man. I was just curious.'

Max gave her a strange questioning look that told her he knew exactly what had happened but like her was respecting Shelly's confidence. 'You won't see him around again now,' he said with meaning. 'His sunbathing days are over.

George is keeping him occupied.'

Sarah felt a load taken off her shoulders. As usual, Max knew exactly what was going on in every corner of his ship and he always dealt with it appropriately.

From then on Sebastian was nowhere to be seen. He didn't appear for meals or in the bar. Nobody mentioned his name. It was almost as if he had never existed and the incident was never referred to.

* * *

Shelly threw herself into work with more than her normal vigour and seemed to be getting more respect from the men she worked with. Slowly she was able to put it out of her mind. Only when she was with Ben did it bother her. She had tried to avoid him for a week or more and felt it came between them like a silent barrier. He had never mentioned it, and neither had she, but he never touched her now and she wondered if he knew what had happened. Not that he wasn't attentive. He spent more and more time with her and seemed overly anxious to keep her cheerful with jokes and stories and bits of gossip. But as the days went by Shelly felt their relationship becoming strained.

One day they were chipping rust off the railings at the side of the ship. Ben carried on chipping and said without looking at her, 'Shelly, do you want to talk about that night? If you don't I'll never mention it again. Malcolm told me. He probably shouldn't have done, but he did.'

She looked up at him. He still chipped away, looking hard at the rails. She went to him and stopped him, but he still looked down at the deck. She lifted his chin and forced him to look at her.

'Kiss me,' she said.

He did kiss her, gently at first, and then he gathered her into his arms and kissed her again.

When they drew apart, his eyes were

full of tenderness. 'I didn't know how you felt after what happened. I didn't want to make it worse.'

'Ben, nothing happened. He threatened me. I fought him off and ran. That's all.'

First he looked concerned, then a smile transformed his face. 'You're a great girl, Shelly.'

She looked into his warm, kind eyes. 'Ben, I do love you.'

      ★   ★   ★

After all the activity in the various ports, Sarah was enjoying the peace of the long sea passage homeward bound. They celebrated Christmas in the middle of the warm Indian Ocean, the men determined to make it as homely as possible by decorating the portholes with spray snow and making a Christmas tree out of a broom handle and coloured paper. There was champagne in the bar at lunchtime and a traditional turkey dinner.

Everyone stood and lifted their glass when Max proposed the traditional toast to wives and loved ones, and Sarah felt a lump in her throat as she remembered all the Christmases they had spent apart and the ones that were to come. Then the men got back to work and it was just another day.

When she wandered out onto the pool deck late that afternoon, she saw Geoffrey standing at the rail looking out to sea, and went to stand beside him. He turned and smiled at her. 'Looking forward to getting home?'

'Yes. How about you? This is a difficult time to be away from your family.'

He swallowed. 'Baby's first Christmas. I wish I could share it with him.'

'I know how you feel. Even without children it's hard. This is the first Christmas Max and I have spent together.'

'I don't think Louise is bothered anymore. At least here I can live with hope. Once we're home I have to face reality.' His voice was full of misery as he stared out over the large expanse of sea.

'Reality may not be so bad. Have you heard anything more from her? Is Simon still doing well?'

'I haven't had a letter since Hong Kong. Nothing in Singapore. That's never happened before. I'm sort of burying my head in the sand and thinking that no news is good news. That's me, I'm afraid — the eternal optimist.'

'There's probably a very good reason. Letters do go astray.'

'I hope so,' he said.

'Another couple of weeks and you'll be with her.'

He smiled and put his hand over hers. 'Thanks, Sarah. For everything. I don't think I could have got through this voyage without you.'

They stood watching dolphins leaping in and out of the waves, but it didn't thrill her now. Her heart was too heavy.

'We all have our problems,' she said.

'Yes, a ship can be a lonely place.'

'Why do you do it, Geoffrey? It's

such a hard life.'

He was thoughtful. 'It's difficult to explain. I suppose it's the challenge. Conquering the elements. A feeling of power, of freedom. Self-sufficiency. When I'm up there on the bridge early in the morning watching the sun rise over the horizon, or when I'm up for'ard with the wind and spray in my face, then I know why I'm here. I can't explain it, I just know it.'

She almost understood. She'd felt the power of the sea, on starlit nights when no light pollution dimmed their sparkling clarity, or when she watched the sky streaked with the lightning of an electrical storm. Even a grey mist over the sea at dawn and the force of waves lashing the decks from a cruel sea moved her. She was beginning to know what drove these men.

★　★　★

Once through the Suez Canal and into the Mediterranean, the air was cooler.

Sarah had been on deck all afternoon, making the most of the sunshine before returning to the cold winter. As darkness began to fall she could feel the ship moving and the sea was becoming quite rough. Then the wind got up and she could hear it whistling round the decks. It sounded as if they were in for some bad weather. As the ship began to move more alarmingly, Max came into the room looking perturbed.

'Max, what's wrong?'

He struggled into his long, heavy bridge coat and then pulled his uniform cap tight to his head. 'Just received a mayday on the bridge. We have to turn the ship around. Some yacht in trouble astern of us. Come up on the bridge with me if you want to.'

There was a feeling of tension on the bridge as Sarah found herself a quiet corner to keep out of the way. Geoffrey scuttled down the ladder to take charge of the men on deck below who were already preparing for action. Rain, wind and waves lashed their fury against the thick glass but in the dimly lit wheelhouse she felt secure.

A desperate voice could be heard every now and then crackling through the radio: 'Mayday, mayday, mayday.' The radio officer was taking bearings from the yacht and relaying them as Max gave continuous orders to the seaman at the wheel to alter course and then, through the ship's telegraph, to the engine room for changes in speed.

'Three men on board, sir,' the radio officer told Max. 'They've lost all power and have no fuel left. Their engine's inoperable. The steering gear has packed in and one of them is in a weak condition. They've been struggling out there for hours.'

Malcolm came in from the port wing of the bridge and checked the radar. The gale-force wind was becoming more ferocious and the ship hitting the waves head-on, causing it to pitch and toss. Sarah tried to keep her balance as she peered through the thick glass. The deck was awash as huge waves broke over its bows and crashed onto the hatches, above which the derricks swung and creaked. Sailors on the deck below were hardly able to carry out their tasks against its onslaught. In the darkness a piercing beam of light cut across the ocean from the *Melbourne* in an attempt to locate the stricken vessel.

After what seemed like a very long spell of high tension, Max ordered dead slow ahead and she could feel the change in the rhythm of the engine. Finally he called for reverse thrust and there were constant communications between the radio room, the men on the bridge and engine room. They'd spotted the yacht and now had to manoeuvre the huge ship close enough to winch the men aboard.

As tension grew on the bridge, Sarah felt she shouldn't really be there and went down the ladder to the deck below. The wind was ferocious and it took all her strength to move against it. Rivets and plates were groaning as the ship rolled and tossed and she staggered from side to side as she slowly made her way along the deck. Sailors were working on the lifeboats, readying them for launching if necessary. She could see Geoffrey, head bent against the elements, his long, heavy coat flapping in the gale and dripping with water.

The ship's searchlights picked out the yacht lurching on the waves ahead of them. Then it disappeared from sight as a giant wave engulfed it and all Sarah could see was white sea foam on the crest of a towering wave. She held her breath. Then the yacht appeared again on the crest of another wave and she let out an involuntary cry of relief.

It must have been and hour or more before the ship began to close in on the yacht, its huge bulk manoeuvring slowly to the exact position of the small craft, and Sarah felt a glow of pride knowing Max had the skill to succeed in such a difficult manoeuvre. Finally they were alongside and she joined some of the galley staff who were leaning on the rail on the port side, looking down at the yacht. She watched in awe as, with great skill, a hoist was lowered down the side of the ship and then, after a heart-stopping few moments, a man was being brought up, the hoist swinging precariously against the ship's side. Once on board the hoist went down again and a second man came up. Then a third. Sarah went down another deck to see if she could help. The men were wet and cold and very distressed. Joe was there and took them inside to be given dry clothes and warm drinks by the stewards.

Sarah returned to the rail to see the abandoned yacht bobbing about below the ship and watched as it crashed against the side and splintered to pieces. First the sides caved in, then the mast swayed, splintered and crashed into the ocean. Eventually the sea took the whole lot away as driftwood.

She stood for a long time watching the waves and the wind, oblivious to the cold and stinging rain until a hand touched her shoulder. It was Geoffrey. He was dripping water from his bridge coat and it was running from his uniform cap into his eyes. 'Sarah, come inside. It's freezing out here.'

She looked at him as if he were an apparition, not feeling that anything about what had happened was real.

'The men are safe. It's okay,' he reassured her.

'But their lovely yacht. It's broken up and gone. The sea can be so cruel.'

He put an arm round her shoulders. 'Come on, let's get you inside.'

In the warmth of the lounge she stripped off her sodden waterproof jacket. Geoffrey disappeared, but was quickly back with a glass of brandy for her. It seemed dazzlingly bright after the darkness of the water. She didn't know where Max was and, as she sipped the drink, she wished she was at home. Geoffrey sat beside her. He didn't speak, but just watched her until he was satisfied she was all right.

'I have to go,' he said. 'Will you go up and have a hot shower? You're shivering.'

'Yes. Thank you.'

'Sarah, don't go outside again. Promise me.'

She looked up into his concerned eyes. 'I promise.'

Then he left her.

* * *

Eventually everyone congregated in the lounge. Joe came in with the three men, now dressed in dry clothes. They looked exhausted and sat at the bar while he got them drinks. Sarah, now warm and dry, hardly knew what to say to them. Then the smaller one of the three spoke to her in Italian.

She smiled at him and he tried again in broken English. Shelly came in and between them they managed to make some sense of what the three men were telling them. They all lived in Genoa and had been collecting the yacht, which one of them had bought. They were on their way back home with it when things began to go badly wrong.

Only the owner of the boat had any sailing experience, and the others began to panic when the storm blew up.

As more men came into the bar the conversation became lively and everyone seemed relieved that no lives had been lost and that the *Melbourne* had done her duty and done it honourably.

14

Decision Time

Sarah watched the coast of Italy recede as they sailed from Genoa on a bright and sunny morning. The three yachtsmen had been landed, grateful to all on board for their safe return home. Max was in high spirits and Sarah supposed it was because they were almost home and he could hand over the responsibility of his ship to another captain for a few weeks and enjoy relaxing at home.

Staring down from the poop deck at the turbulence in the wake of the ship, a great sadness came over her. The first few weeks of his leave would be happy. But as it neared its end she would be constantly aware of the days drifting by until they would part again for months on end. He would go back to his ship and she would be alone. Alone when she came in after a day at school. Writing letters and crossing dates off the calendar. Eating a lonely supper before marking her books and preparing lessons and going to an empty bed. The thought depressed her. She'd been able to put it to the back of her mind during the voyage, but now they were nearing home it loomed large again.

She stiffened and moved away from the rail. She mustn't think this way. They were going home. They had all his leave to enjoy. But it was always the same: however hard she tried to put it out of her mind, there was always this cloud of gathering gloom to remind her that her happiness was transient.

She wandered back into the room and through to the bedroom to change for dinner. Max would be off the bridge soon and they'd go down to the bar for a drink. That would lift her out of this mood.

When he did come down he said he wanted just her company for a while so they took drinks and stood on the deck outside their room, each holding a glass of chilled wine and looking out across a calm sea. It was pleasantly cool, the only sound the gentle lapping of the bow waves across the sides of the ship as she made steady progress through the water, and the screech of gulls swooping and diving in their wake.

Max put an arm around her shoulder as they leant on the rail watching the sun set in a perfectly blue sky, tingeing it with gold. 'Looking forward to getting home?' he said.

'I'm looking forward to having you all to myself again.'

'I know I haven't been able to give you as much attention as I wanted to. It's impossible on the ship. I'm sorry.' His voice was soft with resignation.

She turned to face him. 'Max, I know. And I'm sorry if I expected too much.'

'Would you come on another voyage?'

She was thoughtful. 'Maybe one day. But I have to do something with my own life, Max. I have to go back to teaching. I can't just drift through life waiting for you to come home on leave.' She sighed. She hadn't meant to broach the subject yet.

He turned and looked out across the vast expanse of sea. 'I think the one thing that's come out of this time we've had together is that we understand each other better.'

'I feel that, too.'

'This has been a long and difficult voyage, Sarah. You've seen me in all my moods. What do you feel now about the man you married?' He gave a hollow laugh, then questioning eyes met hers.

For better or worse, this was the only man she would ever want in her life. Wherever he was in the world, however many hundreds of miles separated them, she would support him in everything he did. All she ever wanted was for them to feel as close as they did at this moment. She knew she could do it. She knew she had to do it.

'I love you, Max. I always have and I always will.'

He took the glass from her hand, put

it with his on the table behind them, then gathered her into his arms. 'I do love you so much, Sarah,' he whispered into her hair.

She snuggled into him so that he wouldn't see how watery her eyes had become. Then he kissed her very gently.

★   ★   ★

Max seemed subdued for the rest of the evening until Sarah felt there was something very wrong. They'd been sitting in the room reading, and she knew his eyes were staring blankly at the page. 'Max, what is it?'

He looked up at her but said nothing, his eyes anguished.

'Max, talk to me. Is it something I've said?'

He swallowed. 'In a way.'

She was alarmed. 'What? Tell me.'

He put his book down. 'When we were talking earlier you said you wanted to go back to teaching.'

She frowned. 'Max, if it's going to

upset you that much, then I won't.'

'No, Sarah, that's not it.'

'What, then?'

He sighed. 'Oh, nothing. I think it's a good idea. So long as it makes you happy.'

She was confused. 'Max, what do you want?'

Again the anguished look. 'I want you to be happy.'

She went to him and perched on his knee with her arm round his shoulder and he drew her close.

When she thought about it later, she worried. It hadn't really made sense and she was sure there was more that he hadn't said and all the doubts she'd put aside came flooding back to distress her.

* * *

The ship docked in Liverpool on a wet January morning. Sarah was packed and ready to go. Customs officers were searching the ship in order to give it clearance.

'Have we declared everything we've bought?' Max asked.

'I think so.'

Max grunted. 'You better be sure. It's a serious offence if you get caught smuggling. Not worth the risk.'

Sarah shrugged. 'I'm sure.'

'Phil Pearson from the head office is coming on board. Got word this morning. Very unusual for him to visit the ship on docking day,' Max said.

'Is it because of all the trouble this voyage?'

'I expect so. He'll want a first-hand account.'

'Are you worried, Max?' she asked.

He shook his head dismissively. 'No, why should I be? I dealt with it all, didn't I?'

She smiled at him. 'Of course you did.'

Phil Pearson knocked at the door a moment later. After exchanging a few pleasantries, Sarah left the room so they could get on with their business. She would say her goodbyes to everyone.

Ben was carrying Shelly's bags down the gangway to a waiting car and Sarah watched them kiss goodbye.

'Will you see Shelly again?' she asked as he came back on deck.

'I'm going to stay with her in a couple of weeks.' He smiled shyly at Sarah, then told her he had to get his own bags down.

That was one good thing that had come out of the voyage. Shelly and Ben. Not that it would last. They were very young and both had careers ahead of them. They'd fall in love a hundred times before they settled. But they'd helped each other. Ben was a man now. He had confidence. It was amazing how love could change a person. And Shelly, she'd had a tough time this trip. She was plucky; she was a fighter. But Sarah doubted whether she would have made it without Ben. Those two were good kids. Sarah hoped they'd be all right.

As she watched Ben disappear in his taxi, she saw a woman ease herself out of a car and run clumsily along the quay, dodging the forklift trucks. She was a big young woman, hair blowing in the wind. As she neared the gangway Sarah saw Joe leaping down and then they were in each others arms. It must be Jenny.

Sarah found as many people as she could to say goodbye to, then made her way back. Joe caught up with her. 'Sarah, I want you to meet Jenny.' He introduced the lovely, round, happy-looking girl hanging onto him as if she'd never let him go.

'It's lovely to meet you, Jenny,' Sarah said as they stood in the alleyway. 'Joe's been telling us all about you and how excited he is about becoming a dad.'

'I can't wait to have it,' Jenny said.

Joe couldn't stop grinning.

Sarah smiled at the two of them. 'Will you come back to sea, Joe?'

'I have to, Sarah. Just for a few more trips. I have to get the money together for a house. And this is the only way, especially now I've been promoted to chief steward. I don't want Jen going back to work. I want her to be a real mum.' He gave Jenny an indulgent smile and she beamed back at him.

'I'm so happy for you,' Sarah said. Then she asked them to wait while she got something from the room. Max wasn't around so she went into the bedroom and rummaged in her bag for the teddy she'd bought for Giles. She took it out of its paper bag and cuddled it to her for a moment. Then she took it down and gave it to Joe.

He was delighted and turned to Jenny. 'Our baby's first present.'

As she watched them amble off, Joe whistling and hugging the teddy, a sad and lonely feeling crept over her.

Almost everyone had left the ship now. Sebastian had slunk off down the gangway without a word to anyone. Nancy and Malcolm were still on board somewhere but she couldn't find them. The new crew were joining the ship and everywhere there were trunks and cases. Max would be finished soon then they'd be off. She sat down in the room to wait for him.

At that moment he came striding in and stood looking at her. 'Had a long talk with old Pearson.'

'You look pleased with yourself. What did he say?'

'He congratulated me on how well I'd handled it all. In fact he offered me one of those big new container ships next trip. The newest in the company. Great honour.'

She felt her heart twist. He was already thinking about his next voyage.

'Trips are shorter on those ships. They can be in and out of port in hours. No messing about with general cargo.'

She was struggling to bite back the tears. 'That's good, Max. You deserve it.'

He detected the wobble in her voice and his expression changed. 'Sarah, what's the matter?'

'I don't want to think about you going away again.'

He came to her. 'Sarah, we have to

talk. I've been thinking about what you said. About you needing a life. And you're right. We can't go on like this. I can't expect you to spend your life waiting for me to come home. I can see how unhappy it makes you.'

A cold fear was creeping over her. What was he getting at? Her mind went back to when he'd told her he wished he'd known how she felt about children before he'd asked her to marry him. She'd tried so hard to put it to the back of her mind. Now the memory overwhelmed her again. Was he going to suggest they parted and went their separate ways?

His face was set hard. 'Sarah, I've made a decision.'

A knock at the door interrupted him. Max cursed and told her he'd be a few minutes only and left her.

She stood for several minutes looking at the open door, her heart pounding in her chest, her hands moist at her sides, hardly able to breathe. The minutes went by and he didn't appear again.

Slowly she calmed and began to think more rationally. He'd be back any minute and then they could talk. Whatever the problem, they could sort it. She'd go and find Malcolm and Nancy. She couldn't leave without saying goodbye to them. It would take her mind off what Max had said.

She went up onto the bridge. It was the only place she hadn't looked. But it was Geoffrey she found up there. She'd done her best to avoid him, knowing it would be difficult for both of them.

'I expect you'll be off soon,' she said, trying to keep her voice steady.

He was in the chartroom sorting a cupboard, and straightened up when he saw her. 'Yes, be down the gangway as soon as my relief arrives.'

'How will you get home?'

He looked down at the chart he was folding. 'Louise will pick me up.'

They both turned when they heard voices in the wheelhouse. Louise stood there holding a baby, a small boy beside her. Elegant in a classical grey costume with cream blouse and court shoes, she looked cool and composed. She didn't smile.

Simon rushed up to Geoffrey and he swung him round and round in the air. The baby would have nothing to do with him and began to cry when he tried to take hold of him, clinging to his mother and burying his head in her shoulder. With Simon still clinging to him, Geoffrey put his arm round Louise and drew her to him but she pulled away, leaving the baby in his arms. After a few seconds of screaming and wriggling Geoffrey gave the boy back to Louise and tried to kiss her but she turned her head away. He looked at her in dismay, then moved away, gathered a few papers together and left the bridge with Simon trailing behind him.

Louise hugged the baby close and gave Sarah an apologetic look. Then her face crumpled. 'I'm sorry,' she croaked.

Sarah stood motionless, not knowing what to say or do.

Louise spoke through tight lips. 'How do you tell the person you love that you don't want to be married to them anymore?'

Sarah's heart twisted. Geoffrey had been right. She swallowed and closed her eyes. 'I don't know.' An echo in her heart told her she could be about to find out.

'I can't do it anymore,' Louise whispered.

'But if you love him, surely you can find a way.'

Louise wiped her eyes on the baby's shawl. 'I'm sorry. I shouldn't be talking to you like this. I don't even know who you are. I just felt you might understand.'

'I do understand,' Sarah said.

'I don't want to hurt him but I can't live this life. I don't want to be on my own all the time. I don't want to bring the children up on my own. I can't do it anymore.'

Sarah put a hand on her arm. 'You've had a really tough time this voyage with

Simon being ill.'

Louise, still holding the baby tightly, turned distressed eyes to Sarah. 'But it will happen again. There will always be something. I feel so lonely. And now I've found someone to share my life with, someone kind who really loves me, loves me more than his job and his ship.'

Sarah felt every bit of her heartache and the women exchanged a look of understanding. Louise made her way down from the bridge and left Sarah staring after her. She stood quite still until she felt she had gained control again, more determined now than ever to preserve her own marriage. She wasn't going to let Max do this to her. She would do everything it took to change his mind. She loved him too much to even contemplate losing him.

Eventually she made her way down and stood on deck looking out over the dock, taking a few moments to compose herself and get her thoughts together before going back to their room.

★ ★ ★

Geoffrey came racing along the alley-way and nearly knocked her over. They stopped dead and faced each other.

'I've seen Pearson. I'm to have my command next trip.' His eyes were sparkling with excitement. 'Just imagine, Sarah. Captain Geoffrey Golder, master of my own ship.' He couldn't keep the pride from his voice.

'I'm pleased for you, Geoffrey.' He was going to need that during the weeks ahead to sustain him.

He took both her hands in his and squeezed them gently. Her heart was heavy. They'd been close. Suddenly his face contorted with pain and she knew he didn't want to let her go. 'Sarah, what are we going to do?' His voice was thick with passion.

She was fighting to hold back the tears. 'You have to talk to Louise. I have to talk to Max.'

He looked down at her hands in his. 'I have no future with Louise. You saw that.' His eyes held hers again. 'Could we have a future, do you think?'

She couldn't bear any more of this agony. She shook her head, released her hands and forced her legs to carry her away from him.

What was going to sustain her? She tried to hold her face from crumpling. She knew Max. If he had decided their marriage wasn't working she wouldn't be able to talk him out of it. He made the decisions, and once he had made them there was no turning back. He never changed his mind or compromised.

She stood by the porthole in the room and was so deep in thought she hadn't realised the radio was on. Softly the strains of Sonny James reached her brain: 'Does that little band of gold mean nothing to you?' The tears came pouring down her face as deep inside her she felt love in all its joy and pain.

Max came back into the room. He'd changed from his uniform and was now dressed and ready for off. He took one look at her tear-stained face as she turned to face him. 'Sarah, what is it?'

She turned away from him, struggling to stop the tears coming.

He came closer, took her shoulders and turned her to face him, then lifted her chin and looked deep into her eyes. Her whole world was falling apart. Every sinew in her body was tense. She couldn't breathe. He was going to say it. The thought was unbearable. She loved him so much.

'Sarah, tell me.' He took her in his arms and held her to him.

Through her tears it all came out. 'Max, I love you so much. I don't want to lose you. I'll put up with anything so we can stay together. Please don't leave me.'

He pulled her closer, so close she could hardly breathe. Then he held her away from him. 'Sarah, what are you talking about?' She was sobbing uncontrollably now and he held her to him again. 'Sarah, I would never leave you. I love you. I adore you.'

When she'd calmed a little he took her hands and made her sit down on the settee. He went and closed his door, then came and crouched in front of her and raised her face so that she was forced to look at him. 'What brought this on?'

She tried to compose herself so she could answer him, then it all came blurting out between great, heaving sobs. 'You said we couldn't go on living like this, that you'd made a decision. And you said you wouldn't have asked me to marry you if you'd known how much I wanted a family. And you were so excited about being promoted to this big new ship.' Then she collapsed into his arms and let the tears flow.

He held her until she'd calmed, then pulled away so he could see her face and a smile whispered on his lips. 'Sarah, my love. I didn't finish what I was trying to tell you. This damned ship is a curse. They never leave me in peace for five minutes.' He squeezed her hands and looked deep into her eyes, his face full of love. 'I wasn't excited about that. What I was going to tell you was that I refused Pearson's offer.'

She stared at him. 'What?'

'I told him I'm not going back to sea. That I've done my last voyage.'

'What!' She couldn't take in what he was saying.

'Sarah, I want to be home with you all the time, not just a couple of months here and there . . . ' His voice tailed off.

She continued to stare at him, speechless. Even as joy surged through her, she knew she could not let him do this. The sea was his life.

'Sarah, say something. Tell me I haven't done the wrong thing.'

'Max,' she croaked, 'I can't ask you to do this.'

He held her shoulders and looked deep into her eyes. 'You haven't. And I know you never would.'

A great weight had been lifted from her. She could breathe again. Max wasn't going to leave her. She reached out and pulled him towards her and held him as if she'd never let him go. 'Max, I love you so much. So long as we have each other it doesn't matter where we are. So long as I can feel close to you and know you love me I can cope.'

'But I don't think I can,' he whispered. 'We've never spent this much time together before. I don't think I could bear for us to be parted again.'

She could hardly focus on him now through all her tears.

'You've been beside me through all my moods, all the problems. We've shared all the good bits and the bad. I've shared my innermost fears with you. I've fallen in love with you more every day. I can't imagine not having you there now. I want to be with you, Sarah.'

She burst into a fresh flood of tears and he looked at her in alarm.

'I'm just so happy,' she sobbed.

He shook his head with a smile of relief. 'I shall never understand women.'

'Max, are you sure you want to do this? Your whole life is the sea. You've always said you felt more at home on a ship than anywhere.'

'I used to feel that way. That was before I met you.'

She melted into his arms and he pulled her to him and kissed her gently. 'Sarah, I didn't realise how much I loved you until I thought I might have lost you. When you were in that lifeboat and I didn't know whether you would get back safely I knew then how much you meant to me. I will never forget that feeling.'

'I don't think we were ever in any real danger. It was a lifeboat.' She was laughing now.

'But I didn't know for sure. It was a very bad storm. I should have trusted Geoffrey to get you back safely.'

'Fancy telling him to look after me. Anyone would think I was irresponsible,' she said, her heart full of happiness and love.

'You are,' he said, catching on to her lighter mood. 'You married me, didn't you? So I'm afraid you're stuck with me now, for better or worse.'

She became serious again. 'What will you do?'

'Oh, Pearson suggested a few things. Maybe managing one of these big new container terminals. He's determined not to let me out of his clutches.'

Tears continued to well in her eyes as she looked into the face of the man she loved. 'I can't believe you're not going back to sea.'

'That's right, my love. I'm all yours.'

'Max, I do love you,' she said.

Then he kissed her gently but with great tenderness. 'Not half as much as I love you.'

The phone went and he answered it, then turned to her. 'The taxi will be here in ten minutes, then we'll be off home. I just have one more thing to see to.'

When he left she ambled into the bedroom in a rosy glow to check they hadn't left anything behind. The only thing remaining was the paper bag on the bunk which had held the teddy she'd given to Joe. She picked it up and looked inside. Nothing. It was empty. A great wave of longing caught her unawares. Even now in her happiness, this longing for a baby of her own would not go away. It was still there deep inside. She quickly crumpled the bag and threw it in the wastepaper basket and the pain receded.

She had to conquer this feeling. If Max didn't want children it would be wrong for her to persuade him. Children had to be wanted by both parents. She knew the reason now why it couldn't be. That irrational fear was so deep within Max. She had to accept it.

He was giving up so much for her. There always had to be some give and take in a marriage. Nobody could have everything they wanted in life. Lots of couples didn't have children and were happy. She'd go back to teaching and Max would be there every evening and they'd spend weekends together. She was going home with Max and there would be no more loneliness.

They arrived back at their apartment in a snowstorm. That evening Sarah went out onto the balcony to look at the beauty of the snow-covered trees in the moonlight.

Max came up behind her and put an arm around her waist. She leaned back into him and rested her head back against his chest.

'We have to get a bigger house,' he said.

She looked round at him. 'Max, we have plenty of room for the two of us here.'

'You've never felt at home in this apartment.'

'I don't care where we live so long as we're together.'

'Maybe, but it's not big enough,' he laughed. 'Not nearly big enough.'

'Max, it's quite big enough. You know it is.'

He turned her to face him. In the moonlight she saw how serious his eyes

343

were. 'Sarah, I want us to have children now. I want us to be a proper family.'

She was stunned. Time stood still. Her voice, when she eventually found it, came out as a squeak and then a whisper. 'No, Max, we can't do that. Not the way you feel. You've already done so much for me. I can't put you through that.'

He took her in his arms and rested his head on her hair. 'I couldn't have let you do it alone, not with me the other side of the world. I couldn't have done that. But that won't happen now.'

When she drew away to answer him he put a finger to her lips to shush her. 'Sarah, I'm not afraid anymore. I've found that I can share my worries with you and then they don't seem so bad. I can cope with them.' He pulled her to him and she laughed and cried and her heart was overflowing with happiness.

As they went inside out of the cold night, she was thoughtful. 'Max, won't you miss the sea?'

He handed her a glass of wine as they

stood warming themselves at the fire. 'Sarah, I've been thinking about that, too.' He was silent for a moment, looking at her intently. 'Do you remember when we first met, when we used to visit your sister? We'd take her children for walks in the pine woods and over the dunes onto the beach.'

'We walked miles along that beach watching the waves crashing on the shore,' she said, remembering.

'And do you remember that summer, how we got stuck on the beach one night on the way home?'

She smiled at the memory. 'I remember watching the sunset and feeling very close to you and happy. And we didn't notice the tide coming in and stranding us on a sandbank.'

He laughed. 'We only just made it. I thought we'd have to abandon the car and paddle back.'

'And picnics on the sand dunes,' she said.

'When the sandwiches were always gritty with sand. How could I forget?'

He put his glass on the mantelpiece and took hold of her shoulders so he could look into her eyes. 'Why don't we get a place of our own there, somewhere near the sea? You'd like to be near your sister, wouldn't you?'

She didn't think she could ever be any happier than she was at that moment. 'Max, I'd love it.'

'I'd like our children to grow up loving the sea,' he said quietly.

The radio was playing softly, 'What a Difference a Day Makes'. Max enfolded her in his arms. 'Together now. No more goodbyes,' he whispered into her hair. Then he kissed her long and passionately, and her heart was singing.

THE END